THE GYPSY AND THE GENTLEMAN

SCANDALOUS MISS BRIGHTWELLS

BEVERLEY OAKLEY

AUTHOR'S NOTE

Dear Reader,

I hope you enjoy **The Gypsy and the Gentleman.**

It's a sweet, sensual, racy Regency romp, and it's Book #8 in my *Scandalous Miss Brightwell* series about two matchmaking sisters - Fanny and Antoinette - who first burst upon the stage in Rake's Honour (Book #1) as they recklessly gamble upon fate to make rags-to-riches marriages.

However, the story can be read on its own, and out of sequence.

Happy reading!

BEVERLEY OAKLEY

CHAPTER 1

HENRY STARED OUT OF THE DRAWING ROOM WINDOW, PRETENDING to watch two young boys playing with catapults as they wove in and out of the elm trees that lined the driveway to Quamby House.

Behind him, seated on a Chippendale sofa, his mother was on her favourite topic: Henry's newly elevated status. That, and the suitable marriage he must therefore now make.

"You see, Lady Quamby," his mother droned, "my Henry is a fine proposition even without everything he's inherited. Or, should I say, that he will inherit by month's end, if the physicians are to be believed. Every designing mama is throwing her offspring in front of him." She put down her cup and saucer with a sorrowful sigh. "If that weren't bad enough, Henry refuses to agree to any proposal of a suitable bride put to him by either his uncle or myself."

Henry shifted position, hands on the windowsill, a view of the lovely gardens in front of him, the three chattering women behind him, but forbore to reply. It was as if he wasn't there.

Indeed, he wished he wasn't, just as he would wager Lady Quamby wished she'd not agreed to this little tête-à-tête with

Henry's mother. However, as one of Lord Quamby's god daughters, Lady Quamby would have had no option but to invite them to tea when pressed.

Lady Quamby's other house guest, the young and pretty Mrs Thea Grayling sighed in sympathy. "Fortune hunters. Naturally, you would be on your guard, Mrs Garrick."

Henry didn't turn. Mrs Grayling's boys were currently engaged in a bout of fisticuffs, which was infinitely more diverting than the conversation going on behind him.

When the terms of engagement outdoors appeared to be getting too ribald, he had the excuse he needed to say, "Perhaps I should step outside and separate your sons, ma'am. They appear to be taking their argument to extremes."

"Oh, no need to worry, Mr Garrick, warring is a perpetual state for them, and a great leveller." He heard the smile in Mrs Grayling's voice. "Not that they're both my sons."

Out of the corner of his eye he saw his mother raise her eyebrows as she craned her head to look past Henry's shoulder at the scene to which he referred before she added, "Indeed, I should think not, for the one is a very swarthy lad." Then, as if she feared she might have spoken out of turn, added quickly, "A handsome, confident boy. A relation?"

"A foundling boy."

Interested, Henry watched his mother's response. A swarthy foundling boy, regardless of his age, would not be a playmate of whom she would approve.

He hid his smile as, predictably, his dear mama asked, "And why would you bring a foundling boy all the way here to Quamby House, Mrs Grayling?"

"Oh, the lads are inseparable and my Albert is much more manageable when young Rafe is nearby to keep him company—or in check." Two dimples appeared in Mrs Grayling's cheeks. "We do what we must for a peaceful life. Especially when such a minor act can reap such substantial rewards, not just for ourselves. Rafe is quite an extraordinary boy. Quick, very good with his hands. He's been a member of our household for Albert's whole life."

Henry blinked in surprise. Mrs Grayling spoke of him with as much fondness as she might her own son.

Just as he thought his mama might reveal her prejudices, the golden-haired, vivacious and somewhat scandalous Lady Quamby intervened smoothly. "My son, George, similarly benefited from the company of a foundling lad called Jack, who came here three days a week. Tomorrow we'll be taking all four boys, plus my niece, Katherine, on a picnic. I'm so sorry you won't be here to join us. However—" She paused, and something in the tone of her voice made Henry fix her with the concentration he'd allowed once more to wander.

"What is it, Lady Quamby?"

Obviously, his mother had heard it, too. It was, after all, why she was here: hoping to petition the well-connected, if scandalous countess, for some help in her efforts to augment her forthcoming rise in the world, clinging to Henry's coat tails.

Henry's widowed mother, known throughout the district as the 'redoubtable' Mrs Garrick, had never thought to be the mother of Lord Lomax until several months before when the robust cousin who stood between Henry and an earldom succumbed to a fit of apoplexy he was apparently unlikely to survive.

A tragedy, of course, but bearable since Henry had never met the fellow.

Lady Quamby toyed with a curl by her ear. "Why, I do love any excuse for a little entertainment, and poor Henry's matrimonial troubles have given me an idea."

Henry decided it was time to intervene. He did not trust the look in Lady Quamby's eye. Firmly, he said, "I am confident I can make my own decision in a timely fashion, Mama. One that will please both you and Uncle."

"I'm sure you can manage your own matrimonial affairs, Mr Garrick." Lady Quamby sent a glance at Mrs Grayling, which, to his suspicious mind, seemed almost conspiratorial. "However, do you not wish to be assessed on your personal merits rather than on your pocketbook and the title you appear set to inherit?"

"Naturally," Henry agreed, warily.

"I thought as much." Lady Quamby nodded. "Then what say I host a little gathering for Henry, here? I could select four to six candidates of suitable breeding whom you can get to know much more easily than at the Assembly rooms?"

His mother's brow puckered and Henry himself really couldn't see that this was any less awkward than the usual round of entertainments he attended. Yet the gleam in their hostess's eye suggested there might be more to her proposal.

Knowing Lady Quamby's reputation, he supposed he'd learn of it in due course.

But instead of offering elucidation, Lady Quamby glanced through the window and said, with an affected air of concern, "Henry, I think you're right. Those boys really do need separating. Rafe is giving Albert quite a pummelling. Would you be so kind?"

WHEN HENRY HAD OBEDIENTLY STEPPED out of the room, Antoinette, Countess of Quamby, turned to Mrs Garrick and her cousin, Thea. "The poor boy doesn't know what's in store for him when he arrives in London before month's end. He will be a marked man. I do hope he'll come round to my way of thinking."

"But Cousin Antoinette, it will be no different for him here at Quamby House with six freshly minted debutantes of your choosing, if that's what you're proposing," protested Thea, her sweet face creased with worry. "Henry is such a handsome young man. The young ladies will be falling all over him, regardless."

Mrs Garrick looked about to speak, but Antoinette put up her hand. "I'm not so lacking in imagination that I hadn't thought beyond that," she said. "No, no! Henry will attend, not as Lord Lomax—or the future Lord Lomax, depending on the situation. Rather, he will be…" She looked about her and tried not to reveal her glee, for she knew it really was a marvellous plan.

"What?" Mrs Garrick asked suspiciously, while Cousin Thea had the grace to be patient for, of course, she had enough experience to know that Antoinette was the master of grand plans.

She shifted on the settee, smoothing her mulberry skirts. "Henry will be the dancing master! As plain Mr Garrick, he will be able to study the true natures of each young lady while he tutors them in the dance steps preparatory to their arrival in a few weeks for the London season."

Antoinette watched her guests digest this. Thea looked thoughtful while Mrs Garrick looked concerned.

"But… that is deception."

Antoinette blinked. "Deception? What better way to know the truth, Mrs. Garrick? Surely you see no harm in the truth?"

"Of course not," was the predictable reply. "But my Henry… why, he may not wish to appear as a mere dancing tutor. Such a lowly position. He'll be completely disregarded. It seems a rather… dangerous experiment."

Antoinette hid her frustration. Mrs Garrick was clearly less imaginative than she'd assumed. "All the better for Henry to observe these young ladies' true natures, then. And not an experiment at all." Antoinette felt quite comfortable saying this, for it was indeed her own experience that had inspired the suggestion she'd just made.

The other ladies looked at each other.

Antoinette relaxed a little more, gazing over their heads at the large, well-appointed room, her favourite drawing room of all of those at Quamby House, the magnificent country seat which she'd swapped for the rather precarious succession of lodging houses in which she'd grown up since her noble but impecunious father had prematurely ended his own life.

If anyone knew how to elevate oneself—or someone else—it was Antoinette.

And she did so love to tickle her fingers with a touch of matchmaking. She allowed a smile of reminiscence as she glanced at her cousin. Wasn't Thea one of her success stories?

And now here was Henry: handsome, deserving. He and his mother just needed a little more persuading to allow Antoinette to work the miracles of which only she was capable: finding Henry the perfect wife.

"Recently, while taking the waters," Antoinette told them, "I met a charming young man who was, himself, in a predicament very similar to poor Henry's."

This, she thought, was a suitable little parable to illustrate her point.

"I was at the Assembly Rooms when—let me be familiar and refer to him as *dear Ranulf* for the boy had grown up with no pretensions to grandeur. Well, Ranulf was introduced to me by the Master of Ceremonies. Apparently, the poor boy was attempting to deport himself with the natural ease *your* son, Mrs Garrick, exhibits in company for of course Henry has grown up under the assiduous tutelage of your husband and yourself, together with nannies and tutors."

Mrs Garrick looked perplexed but Antoinette didn't falter.

"This poor young man," she went on, "had recently been elevated to the aristocracy having had no expectation whatsoever of venturing beyond the yeomanry." She nodded. "Yes, you may look shocked indeed, but our birthright is beyond our control and if it should be revealed that one is heir to a title and great estates in the north, as dear Magnus was apprised by the lawyers recently, one is such easy prey for the fortune hunters." She settled herself more comfortably in her chair, adding, "So that is why it was so fortunate for Magnus that he met me."

As Cousin Thea looked blank, Antoinette explained, "I've agreed to ease the young man's way throughout the various entertainments in London that will naturally open their doors to him now that he is the new Lord Ranulph."

"Oh," said Mrs Garrick, frowning as if she doubted the wisdom and sincerity of Antoinette's actions, which was galling since Antoinette was so very buoyed up by the fortnight she was anticipating in the metropolis, squiring—if that was the right word—young Magnus about. She wanted everyone to congratulate her for her good-heartedness. Her guest then made matters worse by adding, "I trust Quamby approves."

"Quamby approves of everything I do," Antoinette said with a breezy air that hid the fact she was bristling inside. "As you know, I have to be in London to represent the family and to do my part chaperoning several god daughters and cousins. And I do all this alone as Quamby's poor limbs are playing up and he has absolutely no wish to be so put upon. Really, I'm doing everyone the most enormous favour!" She hesitated, expecting endorsement from one of her guests.

Instead, Mrs Garrick asked, frowning, "So you will chaperone this… young man from the counties? A… crofter's son or similar? Can he be brought up to snuff? It sounds rather dangerous, if you'll beg my pardon."

And then Thea was adding, "I hope you haven't bitten off too much, Cousin Antoinette, if this young man is so very gauche."

"Gauche? When did I say he was gauche? Why, he is utterly ravishing, if one can use such a term for a young man. Raven dark locks, Mediterranean olive skin and eyes the colour of… seaweed. Interesting green seaweed." Antoinette sought to find the right analogy and was surprised at the lack of enthusiasm from her audience until she realised she had strayed from the conversation, which should have been all about Henry if it were to satisfy Mrs Garrick.

She changed tack. "Believe me, Mrs Garrick, I know what I'm doing. And I love to offer a helping hand to a deserving young man. Especially if he is in danger of being devoured by the young ladies." She managed to stay the urge to giggle and finish with suitable gravity. "I believe my plan to play the role of dancing tutor will ensure Henry has the best possible chance of finding a lady deserving of him. And, really, it will be too diverting for everyone."

Mrs Garrick didn't look amused. "Just as it will no doubt be too diverting to coach Lord Ranulph in the gentlemanly arts so he can be comfortably accepted into society, as is his apparent newfound right. My, my Antoinette, you do play fast and loose with the rules."

"Rules?" Antoinette made a noise to signal her disgust. "Rules are made to be broken. I applaud anyone who can further themselves in society by bending the rules. I did it, and I've suffered no ill."

Cousin Thea gave an audible sigh. "But you're beautiful and you married an earl, Cousin Antoinette. Rules don't matter when you're already on the topmost branch." She glanced at Mrs Garrick, adding, "But they do for the rest of us."

CHAPTER 2

Patiently, Tilly listened to the usual complaints as she created the fashionable coiffure for which Miss Matilda had summoned her.

"You're doing it all wrong, Tilly. I said I wanted the ringlets higher with the pearls threaded through just like last time when Mr Griggs offered me such pretty compliments."

Tilly dropped her hands and settled back on her stool, regarding the young lady who sat frowning at her dressing table. She enjoyed coming to Hamley House, whether for tea and conversation or to do Miss Matilda's hair, even though the young lady was spoiled and demanding. Hamley House was elegant and warm. Mostly warm.

"You're hardly going to win over your man with a scowl like that, Miss Matilda," Tilly warned her. "You look like a bad-tempered ferret with your eyes all squinty when they're usually your best feature. Not that I think Mr Griggs is the right young man for you. But then, you know my thoughts."

Of course, Tilly could not have spoken in such a direct manner if she'd been a lowly servant. Certainly, the humble cottage by the river she shared with her two older sisters was lowly, but the three enterprising women had established a reputation for their herb treatments, successfully treating a variety of maladies that had defied even the local doctor.

And Tilly's talent for fashioning hair had won her Miss Matilda's high regard and, more lately, turned her into a confidante.

Later tonight Miss Matilda was to attend a dinner party hosted by Sir Wylie and his wife, who presided over the village in a rambling Queen Anne manor house perched on top of the hill.

It was Miss Matilda Harcourt's friendship with Miss Jane, a young cousin of Lady Wylie, that accounted for the invitation. However, the recent return to the district of Miss Jane's cousin, Mr Griggs, was behind Tilly's agitation to look her best.

Tilly dipped the tips of her fingers into a bottle of lotion, smoothed it through Matilda's hair, twirled a few strands around the tongs she'd just drawn from the fire, and suddenly Miss Matilda was all smiles.

"I knew you could wreak miracles, Tilly," she marvelled as Tilly executed a few more perfect ringlets. With another of her sudden mood changes, she sighed. "I just wish you could wreak miracles for… that other little matter."

Matilda's mouth curved down once more, giving her a petulant air when she was generally a pretty girl. Spoiled, of course, but Tilly knew how to manage her.

The mention of that 'other little matter' now made Tilly scowl. While she was genuinely fond of Miss Matilda and had reaped the rewards of her patience and wise counsel and honest opinions with a steadily growing pile of cast-offs, Tilly nevertheless considered Miss Matilda had a great deal of growing-up to do before she should consider a lifelong union. That this 'other little matter' revolved around Miss Matilda having set her cap at that arrogant and unworthy popinjay Mr Griggs was a testament to that.

Tilly, at twenty, a few months older than Miss Matilda, did not consider marriage with a man of money and consequence a desirable outcome. For as long as she could remember, her two sisters, Yasmin and Zena—ten and thirteen years older—had warned her that marriage was a contract to beware. In a fashion quite contrary to the mores of the day, they'd encouraged her to go where her heart led her, but had been vociferous and unanimous in their warnings that to bind oneself to one man meant ceding all power to a potential tyrant. Their deceased middle sister, Becca—for Tilly was not a sister by blood—had been a case in point. Becca had followed her heart but had fallen victim to the man who had left her with a child he refused to acknowledge, and whom she'd given away the night before she died.

Perhaps Miss Matilda was one of those women too susceptible to her emotions, like Becca.

Perhaps Miss Matilda simply had no strength to fight an attraction she must know put her at a disadvantage. Tilly, on the other hand, had learnt her lesson young. As a result, she was confident she'd never fall victim to any man again. And she'd never pursue a relationship unless they were equals. Contrary to her sisters' warnings, however, she did wish to marry.

Yes, Tilly believed in following her heart, finding the right man—an equal in every way—and *then* marrying him.

In the brief silence that followed Miss Matilda's lament, Tilly considered the conundrum. If Miss Matilda had fallen head over heels in love, she was too stubborn to heed Tilly's warnings. Perhaps it was best that the attraction run its natural course, which it would do, faster, if Miss Matilda had a week to get to know the young man's true colours.

"It is a shame, then, that you'll miss most of Mr Griggs' visit to the Hall due to the unfortunate timing of Lady Quamby's invitation." A quick reflection on the matter had filled her with inspiration. "You must be so very disappointed."

This lament had the desired effect, for instantly the light dimmed in Matilda's eyes and she looked on the verge of tears.

"Especially when Mr Griggs has been so particular in his attentions these past few days," Tilly added for good measure. That this was true suited Tilly's purposes, for while her poor lot in life meant she needed to be sharp to any opportunity, she also wasn't a liar.

"He has, hasn't he?" Matilda's gaze was forlorn. "Did you not perceive a look of singular pleasure when he took my basket yesterday, after we had chanced upon each other in the town square?"

"Singular," Tilly agreed. "He was delighted to find you in the neighbourhood and now he will be dreadfully cast down to learn that you are leaving so soon to spend the week at Lady Quamby's."

"I don't want to go!" With a sudden wail, Matilda threw back her head and clasped her hands to her throat in her particularly dramatic style. Tilly was used to this, so just fiddled with the brooch on her shawl while she waited for Matilda to let off some of her pent up despair.

"Perhaps it's simply a question of telling your guardian exactly that. He can hardly force you to go where you do not wish to."

Matilda turned tragic eyes towards Tilly. "Yes, he can. And he will! Especially if he comes back from Cornwall and starts asking questions. Miss Taradale will tell him that Mr Griggs is visiting. You know what a snitch she is."

Tilly nodded. Matilda's governess was, in fact, the biggest snitch and tattle-tale Tilly had ever met, and that was saying something.

"I'd have thought your guardian would be only too pleased to welcome Mr Griggs' suit. He's a very acceptable gentleman, isn't he?" The fact that Tilly considered him a popinjay was of no account right now.

Matilda shook her head. "He won't say why he doesn't like him, but it is beyond me why he is so opposed to the idea of my having anything to do with Mr Griggs. I fear that if Mr Collins knew he was in residence, he'd be in his carriage and heading back here posthaste."

"Poor Matilda," Tilly said after a moment's silence. "You and Mr Griggs really are star-crossed lovers. If only you could get someone else to go in your place to Lady Quamby's week of Graceful Instruction, then your guardian would be comfortable under the impression that you were safely at Quamby House and not think to come down here to investigate." For a few seconds, she watched the thoughts she'd instilled flit across her receptive friend's face. Then she rose, adding briskly, "And now I must go."

"Stay!"

Turning at the door, Tilly put her head on one side. She'd planted the seed as successfully as she'd hoped to do.

Miss Matilda swung round on her stool and thrust out her arms in an imploring manner. "What did you say just then? About you going in my place so I could remain here and be courted by Mr Griggs?"

Tilly blinked in surprise. Although this was ultimately what she'd hoped to achieve, she'd had no idea it would quite be so easy.

But she had to pretend it was most definitely not her idea.

"Good lord, Miss Matilda, how could I possibly go in your place?" She grinned self deprecatingly. "Me, a… gypsy girl and you a fine lady?"

"You're not a gypsy girl! It's only what some people say on account of your hair. I'd never send a gypsy girl in my stead!" Miss Matilda was naturally horrified at the suggestion she might commit what would indeed be a criminal act. Changing tack, she gripped Tilly's hand. "But no one would know if you went in my place, would they? Not only do we share the same name, but we are similarly sized."

"And don't particularly resemble each other," Tilly reminded her. "Other than we both have dark hair, only yours is more a hazelnut brown whereas mine is as black as a crow's wing."

Ingenuity quickly replaced Matilda's despair as she countered, "I'll tell Lady Quamby at the last minute that you are my cousin, going in my stead; and ask if she has no objection. She surely will not have. Mr Collins is in Cornwall for the next three months. He'll never know. And Lady Quamby's gathering is only for a few days. You can do this, Tilly. You are the best mimic I've ever known. All those accents. Go on, talk like a lady and show me just how perfectly you would acquit yourself in my place."

So Tilly did, dropping her hand from the door knob and walking slowly and gracefully around the room as she role-played a conversation in tone and sophistication far beyond Miss Matilda's capabilities, even.

"Where did you learn such speech and deportment, Tilly? It wasn't *all* from me."

Tilly resumed her seat with a smile. She really did like Miss Matilda for although the girl was a demanding only child, she was, like Tilly, an orphan, and she was honest in both her conceits and aspirations. And, like Tilly, not ashamed of either.

Tilly shrugged.

"Perhaps it was the short time you spent in Lady Wylie's employ?" Miss Matilda suggested. "Not that you like to talk about that, I know."

Tilly shuddered but forbore to reply.

Miss Matilda leaned forward, clearly hoping to ferret out more. "I saw she cut you in the village last week," she said. "Really, I don't know what you did to upset her so, Tilly, but it was not wise. Lady Wylie is always perfectly lovely to me. And she *used* to like you. Why, she wanted you to attend to her most particularly after she became so enamoured of that tincture of roses cream for the visage that you used to supply her."

Clearly, the reasons for Tilly's abrupt departure from the employ of the squire's wife had been a source of interest to Miss Matilda for some time.

Tilly leaned back against the side of Miss Matilda's bed as she stretched out on the footstool, her legs crossed at the ankles. She smoothed her dark green skirts and grinned at the young lady who was clearly eaten up with curiosity.

"Lady Wylie didn't like to hear what I had to say about a… a fellow – I can't call him a gentleman—she held in high esteem. There. Are you shocked? If you'd asked before, I suppose I wouldn't have told you, for I felt the hurt of her rejection too much." Tilly also wouldn't have told Miss Matilda as the girl was an innocent, and it was wrong to speak ill of others. However, Lady Wylie had been quite vindictive when Tilly had only tried to help her. Guilt did that to a person, though Tilly could understand just how Lady Wylie could have fallen for the wickedly handsome Ranulf Cartwright's charm, for Tilly had fallen victim herself. Not that she intended going into details about this with Miss Matilda.

"What do you mean?" Miss Matilda's eyes were round. "Oh, do tell me, Tilly. Nothing ever happens here. Well, not to me. It sounds like a story. Lady Wylie is married to the squire, though. How could this young man have anything to do with Lady Wylie? What do you mean? Surely—?"

"I mean nothing other than I thought Lady Wylie was too trusting of this young man who I knew was not who he said he was, only she wouldn't believe me. Enough of that, though." Tilly rose. "So, if you intend to ask Lady Quamby if your *cousin* can go in your place, you'd better do that today." She raised one eyebrow in collaboration. "The House Party—or week of Graceful Instruction—is only a few days away, which doesn't leave too long to brush up on my social graces. Are you sure you're not afraid I'll dishonour you?"

"You're too clever and everyone likes you too much that they'd forgive the occasional slip-up," Miss Matilda said with an air of distraction that suggested she was dreaming of Mr Griggs once more.

"Well, I'll go, then," Tilly said, rising. "I'm sure Mr Griggs will think you look beautiful in your new pink dress. I think the addition of the embroidered roulade around the hem was just the thing."

"You have such impeccable taste, Tilly!" Miss Matilda said with renewed enthusiasm. "I'm so glad you suggested the roulade. I can always trust you." She turned and hurried to her wardrobe. "Before you go, I nearly forgot to give you these," she said over her shoulder as she opened the door. "Both are from last year, so I can't possibly wear them when I go to town in a few weeks, but they'd fit you if you want to wear them at Lady Quamby's."

"Why, thank you," said Tilly as she received the armful of dresses Miss Matilda had retrieved from the bottom shelf. She stroked the soft, lustrous fabrics with delight. "They look as if they've hardly been worn, but if they are so recognisably 'last year' then I shall happily go as your poor relation, which is for the best." Grinning, she held up a pale blue sarsenet intricately embroidered with gold thread.

"That was my favourite, but is now so terribly dated, I'm afraid," Matilda lamented.

"Which is only to the good since advertising my impoverished unsuitability puts me out of contention to the gentlemen of the ton." Tilly stroked the gown, thoughtfully. "Yasmin insisted on reading my future and, of course, I am to meet the man of my dreams at Quamby House."

With shining eyes, Matilda gripped her forearms. "Don't sound so sceptical. Yasmin is a true soothsayer!"

"Yasmin only says what she thinks will earn her a few more coins." Tilly chuckled at Matilda's predictable outrage. "Or a robust response from me to fund her amusement."

Looking smug and decided, Matilda shook her head. "No Tilly, the crystal ball does not lie. I predict that before the season is over, we both will be living the lives of which we've long dreamed: Two orphans who have finally found a place to call home with the man of our dreams."

CHAPTER 3

IT HAD TAKEN A GOOD DEAL OF PERSUASION ON THE PARTS OF both Henry's mother and Ladies Quamby and Fenton for Henry to agree to the plan.

Play the role of dancing master? It had seemed an extreme, if not demeaning, way to proceed. However, when the first two young ladies to arrive for Lady Quamby's illustrious event cast barely a glance in Henry's direction, he realised that no better plan existed if he was to escape his mother's attempts to marry him off before he was ready.

Not that he *was* ready, he'd recently decided, though a year ago, the idea of marriage had had its temptations. But a year ago he'd not been anywhere within sniffing range of a title, much less the inheritance that would allow him a freedom he could not have imagined.

When his cousin had fallen suddenly ill, and Henry was publicly declared his heir, Henry had, for a brief time, enjoyed the attention as his mother threw herself into finding him a wife 'worthy of him', as she'd put it.

However, he'd soon grown weary of being the focus of every mama in the country with a daughter to marry off.

Standing by the same drawing room window in Quamby House at which he'd stood two weeks earlier, he surreptitiously observed the three young ladies and two gentlemen who had arrived during the past hour.

The two young men—both gangly and awkward—spoke to each other with earnest intensity by the fireplace, while the young ladies gathered in a serious self-conscious huddle in the centre of the room.

Near the door, Lady Quamby and her sister, Lady Fenton, were in conversation with an older woman who had just deposited her daughter, whom she was instructing on how to behave for the next few days.

There'd be no dispute that all these freshly minted debutantes were pleasing to the eye, but none had excited an instantaneous interest.

Well, Henry would not be bound by whatever transpired during the week, however, it would be a diversion to see how differently young ladies behaved when they did not see him only for his outward worth.

The soft chatter was disturbed when Lady Quamby clapped her hands for silence as she glided into the centre of the room, the light from the decorative mullioned window making her golden hair gleam. Lady Fenton, the older, dark-haired sister, had just exited the room, making Lady Quamby, who was older than these young chits by a decade and a half, the most striking of the company, thought Henry—if one preferred blondes. Which he did not. Raven haired sirens had always caught his eye.

With a smile and an expansive gesture that highlighted her graceful arms and swanlike neck, Lady Quamby began. "Almost everyone has arrived though we are missing one gentleman who has been delayed on the road, and one young lady still to grace us with her presence. Hopefully, neither is the victim of a broken axle or footpads, but as we have not been apprised of their arrival time, let me in the meantime explain what the next marvellous few days have in store!"

The two brown-haired lasses looked excited, while their more beautiful companion, another ravishing blonde named Miss Laidlaw, showed no outward emotion. She glanced at Henry before her eyes slid away to focus on gangly Mr Snape for one brief, disdainful moment.

"My sister, Lady Fenton, and I are delighted to host our first Graceful Accomplishments week here at Quamby House," said Lady Quamby. "Dancing and conversation are important components of anyone's introduction into society, and we have found three obliging gentlemen to partner our four young ladies, besides our dancing tutor, Mr Henry Garrick who has made a special journey here from his home far away near the Scottish border. Indeed, our accomplished dancing master is the most sought-after in the land."

Henry raised his eyebrows in surprise as he acknowledged the interest of the rest of the company. However, once the young ladies had finished looking him up and down as if he were an interesting specimen, but nothing more, while the gentlemen dismissed him with barely a glance, Henry wasn't sure he liked the sensation of being so below notice.

Still, he reconciled himself, what better way to evince the genuine regard of a lady if he was not the wealthy young Lord he would become?

Lady Quamby offered the company a satisfied smile before saying, "And now, please would the gentlemen introduce themselves to the company."

The two young men—Mr Reggie Snape and Lord Oxenholme—were at first tongue-tied by the attention before red-haired Reggie regaled the company with a checklist of the estates and houses he would inherit, while Lord Oxenholme spoke with enthusiasm of his love of horse-racing, gaming and 'the ladies, of course!'.

"And now it is your turn, Mr Garrick," said Lady Quamby. "Your calling as a dancing master has taken you all over the country. There is none better than you from whom our lovely young ladies can learn their steps."

"I'm not sure that's true, Lady Quamby," Henry said, feeling awkward as he realised he'd once lost a wager to Lord Oxenholme during a long, whisky-fuelled night at some gaming hell he couldn't quite recall. Hopefully Lord Oxenholme did not recognise him, though it appeared he did not. Henry had only spent one week in the country's capital. Money, at that stage, had not permitted a longer stay after his disastrous initiation at the gaming tables. Since then, he'd adopted a more sober approach to life.

"Why, Mr Garrick, you are too humble. My sister and I have been so eager to secure your expertise since we learned of your return from the Continent where you became practised in the styles favoured by the noble courts of Europe." She sent a knowing smile to the company assembled as she added, "We are so delighted that Mr Garrick has agreed to show you fortunate young ladies how to acquit yourselves in the manner of a princess before Mr Garrick retires to his main residence in Hampshire after the novelty of passing on his expertise." She turned to Henry. "Is that not so?"

Really? thought Henry, careful not to frown, for he should have expected Lady Quamby would manage the lie on his behalf.

So, he was to be a gentleman of modest means, rather than a lowly dancing tutor. That did make matters more palatable—if he had indeed been intending to use Lady Quamby's little experiment as a means of selecting a wife.

Which he decided he was not—though he was quite happy to humour her. For surely it could not be too great a hardship to teach four pretty girls to dance?

Patiently, he waited for Lady Quamby to finish. The music,

she told them with a flourish, was to be supplied by her very own sister, Lady Fenton, who was as accomplished on the pianoforte as Mr Garrick apparently was upon the dance floor.

"And so, ladies and gentlemen, as you are all proficient in the usual cotillions and quadrilles, our purpose today is to teach you the waltz—"

The collective titter was truncated by the whoosh of the double doors as they were thrown open to admit a tall, raven-haired, broad-shouldered gentleman with a fine head of carefully coiffed curls and a three-tiered swirling cape which performed with theatrical aplomb as the newcomer offered his apologies to his hostess.

Henry was amused by the interest occasioned by the older and more dashing Mr Fortescue when quick dainty footsteps across the parquetry floors heralded a flushed and very pretty young lady in a white sprigged muslin gown and poke bonnet who said with no trace of embarrassment for being the obvious centre of attention, "Lady Quamby, what a pleasure to meet you. I am Miss Tilly Manners from Hertfordshire and I do appreciate you accepting me in place of my cousin, Miss Harcourt, who was unable to attend."

As Miss Manners sent an interested look about the room, with not the slightest trace of coyness, Henry felt the breath catch in his throat and a lot more besides as she levelled a smile upon him, adding, "And who is the dancing tutor? I'm afraid I missed the introductions."

Even Lady Quamby looked surprised by the confidence of the newly arrived and supposedly not-yet-out young miss. In Henry's experience, young ladies had great difficulty responding with anything other than stammered responses to carefully directed questions accompanied by furious blushes.

Miss Manners clearly did not need some of the instruction that Lady Quamby had devised to benefit her young charges.

And she was suddenly a great deal more interesting than her

fellow debutantes as she took up position within their ranks, adding to her hostess, "And I implore you to pull me up if I do run on as I am an inveterate chatterbox. It's one of the reasons I was sent here when Cousin Matilda couldn't come."

"Indeed, Miss Manners," said Lady Quamby, "you are right that to talk too much is as much an impediment to a young lady getting along in society as is being unable to respond with more than stammers and stutters."

She looked about to say more but Miss Manners interrupted, with an earnest look as she brushed back a strand of her glossy coal black hair that had escaped the confines of her bonnet, "And what is the principal reason we are here, Lady Quamby? I'm afraid I was despatched in rather a hurry and told merely that it would be a benefit to me to learn to deport myself with more grace upon the dance floor and to know when—and when not—to speak."

Henry didn't realise how much he was enjoying himself until he heard a stifled gasp. He glanced up and noticed that Miss Laidlaw, the self-confident young blonde, was sending Miss Manners a somewhat rancorous look, as if she felt that Miss Manners was trespassing beyond the bounds of propriety for speaking up at all.

Henry hid a smile as he observed the changed dynamics since the arrival of the more confident Miss Manners and older and more dashing Mr Fortescue, who clearly thought himself a cut above the rest.

The next few days, he thought, could be more entertaining than he'd anticipated.

AFTER INTRODUCTIONS in the ballroom and then some quiet time in Tilly's new bedchamber—the most luxurious room in which Tilly had ever been accommodated—Tilly came downstairs to join the other young ladies, armed with a piece of embroidery Matilda had given her for the purpose, and which she worked at for a frustrating half an hour.

She'd tried to initiate conversation with Miss Laidlaw who'd offered nothing but monosyllabic responses and Miss Dorley who'd sniffed and said, "Mmm, very nice," three times to observations that Tilly felt had the potential to open up an illuminating discussion on matters of the day.

For Tilly really was very interested in matters of the day and of the opinion of the kinds of people who influenced the lives Tilly and her kind lived. It was one reason for turning matters to her advantage so that she could come here in Matilda's stead.

That and a couple of other compelling reasons, which she could not, of course, divulge.

The needlework was becoming exceedingly tedious so when the arrival of a couple of the gentlemen caused a slight stir, she was quick to volunteer to go for the walk that was proposed, jumping up with what she realised was much too unseemly haste as she declared, "It's far too fine a day to moulder inside and I am fagged to death with stitching this insufferable daffodil. Where are we going, Mr Garrick?"

He levelled a long look at her before the corners of his mouth turned up and he said with a gallant bow, "Wherever you would like, Miss Manners."

It was then that she realised that every other female in the room was regarding her with open hostility, and her hostess with amusement.

Lady Quamby now rose and said, "Naturally, the pair of you can't venture out together, alone. Let us make up a party. Ladies, shall we go upstairs and fetch shawls and change our footwear. We'll meet on the portico in ten minutes."

Ten minutes later and Tilly was the very first to be pacing up and down the stone walkway, champing at the bit to be out and enjoying the good weather.

Actually, it wasn't very good for the sky was grey and the grass was damp but Tilly was unused to be being closeted indoors for long. Since she could remember, she'd been sent off by her sisters on all manner of expeditions to deliver herbs and various herb concoctions to the families about the area.

It was how she'd first come to know Matilda after Matilda had become a slavish consumer of Tilly's sisters' famous Dandelion Dew and other skin softening products.

"Miss Manners, I see punctuality is to be added to your list of accomplishments."

It was the very handsome dancing tutor, Tilly noticed with pleasure, appearing from around the back of the house —alone, she was even more pleased to notice. The other young ladies seemed vacuous and unintelligent on world affairs, so not likely to add anything to the tone of the conversation but this Mr Garrick, being a few years older— perhaps five or six-and-twenty—no doubt had a litany of adventures to recount.

And there was nothing Tilly liked more than an adventure.

"I'm not sure punctuality can be called an accomplishment, but I am weary of being indoors. In fact, I cannot bear to be closeted inside for too long." She smiled at him, liking the way he responded with a nod of agreement, his eyes crinkling with good humour when she added, "I hope the others are not too long for it's chilly standing here when we could be striding across the fields."

"A young woman of action, as well. That is unusual," he said. "So, you enjoy the outdoors?"

"A great deal more than sewing my sampler and listening to gossip." She shaded her eyes to peruse the landscape, adding, "A rain shower looks headed this way, and I'd much rather be in the middle of our walk than be told we should postpone it. What say we stride on ahead, Mr Garrick?"

He raised his eyebrows. "I think we cannot do that, for all

that I would enjoy your exclusive company, Miss Manners, and have no doubt that we shall deal famously together."

Tilly contemplated him with a frown. "Your tone suggests – I suppose, correctly – that what I suggested is not seemly. As to whether a young lady can learn if she would indeed 'deal famously' with a gentleman, I think that, sadly, she must have committed too much to the relationship to be allowed to withdraw honourably if indeed it proves that she does *not* deal famously with the gentleman in question." She sighed. "So many rules, Mr Garrick." She glanced longingly at the empty, beckoning fields as she heard chatter in the vestibule and said, "Company is on the way. Shall we make a start? I'm sure it wouldn't be considered a sin if we are only a few yards ahead of the pack."

"A walk in good company, with *others*, even if they are a little distant, is definitely no sin," he reassured her.

"Yes, of course I know there must always be others in attendance, though I do worry that I am not entirely sure at which point enjoying another's company is considered a sin," Tilly said, making her way down the stairs.

"I think we can cast aside our worries for the meantime and find something else to talk about," he said, walking abreast of her now as the others, who appeared companionably in conversation within their own group, brought up the rear.

Tilly drew in a sustaining lungful of air and added, "Like how gentle the countryside is compared with the rugged cliffs I call home. Though you mistake me if you consider I'm an inveterate worrier, for indeed my capacity for risk is considerably greater than my companions', I'd wager," Tilly said. "My worry is that I might bring opprobrium upon those whom I represent through ignorance, for it was impressed upon me, prior to my making this visit, that I must strive to temper my lack of concern for the boundaries of proper behaviour. Having no parents, there are many who consider I've been allowed to run a little too free."

He sent her an interested look.

"I'm sorry. You are an orphan? Like Miss Harcourt, your cousin? Lady Quamby said Miss Harcourt's guardian was a gentleman who is currently spending three months in Cornwall while leaving his ward, who is to be presented in a few weeks, under the tutelage of her governess."

"Yes, Mr Collins is a single gentleman far more interested in rocks and fossils than in bringing up his niece though he has striven to do his duty by employing others to guide my cousin towards what I suppose he'd consider is the pinnacle of her success: a good marriage." Tilly raised an eyebrow and sent him a smile, adding before he could comment, "As we live close, we often bear one another company."

This was true enough, Tilly thought. Although Matilda was often superior in her attitude to Tilly in public, she did seek Tilly's advice in private. Particularly, these days on matters pertaining to Mr Griggs.

Or, rather, not her opinion, but Tilly's crystal ball readings of Mr Griggs.

Since Tilly had been young, she'd been fascinated by how her sisters could read the futures of those who paid for such knowledge.

The heavy, clouded crystal ball that was kept shrouded in a sequined and beaded cloth in a dark cupboard would be brought out and consulted with much mystical ceremony.

Tilly, herself, had been instructed in its use, but the truth was that she had never set much store by its prognostications.

There'd been too many instances where the prophecies had simply been unfounded or never come to pass. Not that there wasn't always some excuse or reason why this was so. Tilly had learned not to refer to it. Her scepticism did not sit well with the oddly assorted 'family' who'd brought her up and whom she loved.

So, she simply copied the other womenfolk and, with Miss Matilda, steered her towards making decisions which Tilly thought were the most sensible in that young lady's situation.

She looked up to see Mr Garrick regarding her with interest, and Tilly felt an unexpected jolt of gratification. The dancing tutor was an engaging young man, both in looks and manner.

"Well, Miss Manners, I must say—" he began, but was prevented from saying what he must when Tilly thrust out an arm to point at a couple of children romping in the grass, and cried, "Who are those boys?"

She squinted, trying to observe their features from this distance, while an oddly excited feeling coursed through her.

"The two fair-haired lads are the sons of Lady Quamby and Mrs Grayling," replied Mr Garrick.

"And the dark-haired boy?" Already Tilly was marching towards them, determined to see for herself what possible resemblance there might be to anyone she knew. She'd not told her two sisters and aunt where she was going for these few days, but she well remembered the family feud over the babe who'd been spirited away in the dead of night by the sister who'd died shortly afterwards.

Not that any of them were really family by blood, though they were the only family she knew.

"I really couldn't say." Mr Garrick hurried after her. "Miss Manners, I think the rest of the party is calling us to join them."

"Then you go and join them, Mr Garrick. I want to talk to the boys." Tilly waved him away, her heartbeat ratcheting up several notches as she beheld the three youngsters whom she guessed were aged about ten.

"Boys!" she called, and they swung round, blinking in surprise to be addressed by a grown-up whom they obviously perceived threatened their outdoors fun for they immediately turned tail and bolted back towards the house.

Tilly retraced her steps to find Mr Garrick frowning at her a short distance away. She supposed her behaviour might seem odd to him, but she didn't care. "Could he be one of the foundling children?"

"I'm told he is, yes. Though he is well dressed for a foundling child." Mr Garrick regarded them thoughtfully. "I've heard that the Graylings showed a kindness to the lad who is a playmate for their son, Albert." He offered her his arm.

Tilly had been thinking about the boy but the moment she tucked her hand into the crook of his elbow, a jolt of awareness ran through her and she blinked up at him, surprise evident in his own gaze.

And then the rest of the walking party were upon them, Miss Laidlaw saying, archly, "I say, Mr Garrick, won't you join Miss Dorley and myself who have never waltzed and, to be frank, are rather anxious about it."

"Indeed, you must allay Miss Laidlaw's concerns," Tilly said, relinquishing Mr Garrick's arm without a thought, as if he would obviously wish to discuss a dancing-related concern rather than squire her about.

Yet, she didn't think she'd imagined the gleam in his eye as they'd locked gazes.

Not at all. A warm, fluttery feeling was filling her with sensations she hadn't experienced for some time, but Tilly knew when to bide her time. She'd not be accused by Miss Laidlaw and her ilk of having designs upon the handsome dancing tutor when clearly Miss Laidlaw and her ilk considered themselves a cut above Tilly.

Which was true, though they needn't know to what extent.

Tilly brought up the rear, alone, and didn't miss the look Mr Garrick sent over his shoulder as he found himself flanked by Miss Laidlaw and Miss Dorley.

Tilly, meanwhile, was suddenly thrown off guard by finding herself walking alone with no lesser personage than Lady Quamby who said, easily, "Tell me what has indisposed your cousin, Miss Manners? I haven't seen Matilda in many months but she has always been robust."

"Yes, rarely a day of illness in her life. But she hasn't been feeling quite the thing. I do hope it hasn't inconvenienced you for me to have come in her stead. I am grateful that you responded so kindly to her request."

Lady Quamby sent her a considered look. "I daresay you bring a little colour to the company. You are not what I'd have expected of Miss Matilda's cousin, knowing her late mother." Sweeping her with a look that was not as appraising as Tilly would have liked, she went on, "Miss Matilda certainly has not your confidence in public."

"She is very different in private," Tilly responded.

Lady Quamby inclined her head. "True enough. Matilda does know how to get what she wants." She pressed her lips together as if she might have said more, then added, "I daresay she wants to ensure her strength for her London debut. Like most young ladies her age, she'll be hoping to find a husband in the next few months. Which is why I'd hoped she'd grace us with her presence."

"Matilda has already found a young man she wishes to marry," Tilly said, interested to see how this would register with Lady Quamby.

Her hostess hesitated. "Are you suggesting that is the real reason she is not with us?"

Tilly nodded.

Lady Quamby's lovely face took on heightened colour and Tilly tried not to show her discomfort as the grand lady went on, "So you are here because Matilda thought you'd benefit in her stead? Only she did not wish her guardian to know the truth?"

Tilly cleared her throat. "Perhaps." Suddenly, she was on unstable ground. Lady Quamby was skilled at ferreting out the information she wanted, but Tilly was not one for keeping secrets.

Well, she'd keep the secret of her identity, but only to a degree. She wasn't here on some dramatic subterfuge. She glanced up at the back of Mr Garrick's head: a Brutus cut, she believed it was called, with his dark brown curls cut short at the sides and fullness on top.

A dancing tutor would need to cut a fashionable figure, she decided.

She'd enjoyed talking to him. As soon as the two young ladies were finished their questions, she was sure she had far more diverting conversation with which to compensate.

"You like Mr Garrick?"

Tilly blinked to see Lady Quamby regarding her.

"I do," she nodded.

"So do the other young ladies."

"But they are heiresses, perhaps, or at least have dowries and consequence that would be wasted on a dancing tutor." Tilly shrugged. "Even if they think him a fine match, their papas will not."

"You are a shrewd piece." Lady Quamby sized her up. "Or rather, not shy to voice the obvious when more demure young ladies would have known to keep their silence."

"A poor relative learns to read the situation and I have never been able to hold my tongue."

Lady Quamby sniffed. "Mr Garrick has a private income. He is rather more than a lowly dancing tutor."

But he would not be here in the capacity of a dancing tutor if he had the pocketbook to entice an heiress. And Tilly was not an heiress, she thought with satisfaction, lavishing another look upon the back of Mr Garrick's handsome head.

She was only too delighted when the two young ladies with

Mr Garrick paused to attend to something said by their hostess, enabling Tilly to slide into the vacuum and say, "I trust you have satisfied their questions on the waltz, Mr Garrick. I, by contrast, have nothing of interest to remark upon except the weather and the way that cloud looks like a tremendous dragon, don't you think?"

"I don't have your fanciful imagination, Miss Manners. Though now you mention it, I would say it rather resembled a great slavering beast, more like a minotaur. I don't know where you might you have seen a dragon."

"In my part of the world, the rugged cliffs and caves are the home to more than just dragons. We have smugglers and pirates, whereas this gentle landscape looks like it would harbour nothing villainous. Unless you have seen a dragon else-where than in the clouds, Mr Garrick?"

He raised a brow. "I think perhaps you know I do not believe in such things."

"Not in dragons? Or faeries? Or the ability to see into the future?" Tilly pretended surprise. "Why, my family hold very much to such things. I think you and I have little in common, in that case, and Mr Garrick and I should leave you to Miss Dorley and Miss Laidlaw, who are clearly far more diverting than myself."

She made as if to leave, but he reached out his arm and clasped her wrist, drawing her back to his side at the same time as flicking a glance at the rest of the party. "I think you are the most diverting young lady here and would be very disappointed if you left." There was lazy assessment in his gaze and Tilly's heart did another little lurch. He raised an eyebrow. "No, I don't believe in these so-called dragons and faeries... but you're welcome to try and convince me."

Tilly smiled. "Perhaps when we are on the dance floor, it will take your mind off the insult to your toes, which I am sure to inflict upon you, or the lovelorn looks the young ladies will send you. Yours must be a delightful calling. I'm sure you break hearts wherever you go, Mr Garrick. It must be exciting, travelling about the country. Though lonely, perhaps?"

They'd stopped to wait for the others to catch up.

"It's never lonely when I am in company as diverting as yours, Miss Manners," he said. "But lately I've felt a desire to swap my nomadic life for something more permanent." He paused. "Perhaps I'll have to consult you with your expertise with the crystal ball so you can forewarn me of the dangers and possibilities ahead."

Now it was Tilly's turn to hesitate in order to give him the considered answer that was required. "I think you know, Mr Garrick, that I was only teasing when I spoke of dragons and faeries and crystal balls," she said. "To tell you the truth, I believe your future is what you make of it."

CHAPTER 4

THE BALLROOM WAS ENORMOUS FOR SUCH A SMALL PARTY. A cluster of young ladies huddled near one of the pillars; the two young men were in deep conversation with one another.

And Miss Manners, whom he immediately sought, was talking to Mr Fortescue.

It shouldn't have bothered Henry, of course, but he'd wanted to find her alone and abandoned so he could draw her onto the dance floor as he began the lesson.

Instead, Miss Laidlaw was putting herself forward, and it would have been ungentlemanly of Henry not to have accepted her as his partner.

Now Henry was slowly explaining posture, movements, all the mechanics of the dance as if he were the arbiter when, in truth, he knew little more than anyone else who'd been dancing the waltz for as many years as he had.

Lady Quamby was on the sidelines, smiling on; her sister was at the keyboard. The two shy young men looked awkward while Miss Manners, in the arms of Mr Fortescue, recounted some, no doubt diverting, anecdote with sparkling eyes.

Henry wished she could have been recounting it to him.

As she glanced up and saw him from above her partner's shoulder, she smiled.

And it caught him in the solar plexus. Her smile was so artless and unfeigned. A smile of appreciation and... admiration?

Miss Laidlaw said something, and he had to ask her to repeat it.

The warm June sun beat through the windows and Henry felt the perspiration seep into his neck linen. Lady Fenton played on.

And all Henry wanted to do was escape and plunge into the cool waters of the nearby river.

At least that might reorient himself, for in this hot, close ballroom, he felt dangerously out of his depth.

THE DANCING ENDED, the ladies rested.

And then it was time to stitch companionably in the drawing room.

Tilly had never been more bored in her life. The daffodil embroidery with which Matilda had saddled her was going to send her screaming round the bend, as Yasmin, her elder sister, used to say.

The company was tedious in the extreme, and the heat threatened to send her to sleep.

What she'd like was a refreshing dip in the river which—she glanced up as movement through the window caught her eye—was exactly what Mr Garrick had in mind.

Yes, there he was, alone and striding across the lawn with purposeful steps. Not the gait of a man enjoying a country ramble. He didn't seem that sort of fellow, either.

But a fellow on a mission.

And he was going to the river to cool down, which was

exactly what Tilly wanted more than anything.

And why not?

She straightened, glancing about at her fellow stitchers. "I'm running out of thread. I'll go to my room now," she said. A couple of her companions nodded, as if it was of no account. Which it wasn't.

"Actually," she amended, "I think I'll have a rest. The dancing lesson earlier was quite strenuous."

Out in the fresh air, with a shawl about her shoulders—with which she could use to dry herself later—Tilly felt a rare sense of freedom.

Lord, if this was how stifling Matilda's life really was, then Tilly wanted none of it. What better way to discover how good she had it than to have to step into Miss Matilda's shoes for a few days?

That said, Matilda had more freedom than most of her contemporaries, though perhaps having a disinterested guardian wasn't as good as having a tumble-down cottage full of affectionate sisters.

Well, gratuitous, grasping and affectionate. Tilly loved the two women who'd brought her up, but she had no illusions as to how far they'd go to get what they wanted. Self-interest trumped sentimentality. She'd always known that.

It wasn't difficult to ascertain Mr Garrick's location. The splashing of water and the occasional groan of appreciation lured Tilly to the precise spot, and she'd been standing on a gnarled tree root for some time before he blinked open his eyes and found he was the object of her interested study.

"Good lord, Miss Manners! You shouldn't be here!" were his first words, which Tilly thought rather odd. Why shouldn't she? She roamed freely about the countryside when she was in familiar territory. But there seemed to be an endless list of things nicely brought up young ladies didn't do. Matilda had schooled her in many of them during the few days of coaching Tilly had received beforehand.

"I swim at home, Mr Garrick," she said. "And when I saw you were obviously going to swim, I thought it a splendid idea."

He looked alarmed. "But… you can't swim *here*. Not alone, and certainly not alone with me. Why, I have no—"

He stopped suddenly, and Tilly supplied, "No clothes on? But of course. I'd not have expected anything else, for how else is one to swim? And that is why I'll ask you to avert your eyes while I undress and enter the water a little further upstream." She frowned. "I'll keep my distance, if that's what you wish, but I didn't think you'd dislike the idea so very much."

"I… don't!" He shook his head, and seemed unable to formulate a proper sentence until he said, "What if you were followed?"

"I don't think I was, and—even though I don't believe that would present a problem—I can remain under water quite some time, if that's what you'd prefer." She drew off her shawl and sat on it while she pulled off her walking boots. "There really are so many rules, aren't there? I find it quite difficult to keep them all in my head."

"But, Miss Manners, it's not very hard. Young ladies and young gentleman must not be alone together unless—"

"Unless marriage is the intention?" Tilly asked, now taking off her stockings, one by one, and draping them neatly over a low-hanging tree branch. "But marriage isn't the intention, is it, Mr Garrick? We've only just met."

"But… if someone were to find us together like this, then I would be obliged…"

Tilly, having just pulled her gown over her head, rose to her feet in only her chemise and regarded him steadily. "Then I promise not to accept."

"But there'd be your reputation…."

Tilly shrugged. "I don't want to get married just yet, if that's what you are worried about. And I'm not too bothered about my reputation. I'm not going to London where it will be under scrutiny. And right now, I'm very hot." She smiled, hoping she'd allayed his concerns. "I'm sorry to have upset you, Mr Garrick, and I'm certainly very happy to move further upstream. It's just that the house is so close and I knew we were within an easy walk of the river. Like as not, the others will make up their own bathing party a little later."

"I hardly think so, Miss Manners, for it is not the thing in our part of the world." His tone relaxed as he went on, "But, please, now that I have laid out all my objections and you are still of a mind to swim, I would be delighted if you joined me. I promise to avert my eyes."

"Wonderful!" Tilly said, pulling her chemise over her head and, with a flick of her wrist, sending it to join the pile of clothes on the river bank. "Sadly, I think it wouldn't be considered seemly to wet my hair before dinner, so I won't jump in. But... oh my goodness, this is just the refreshment I needed," she finished as she stepped off the raised riverbank and into the depths, finding the water level to be just above chest level.

"There, Mr Garrick. You didn't look, did you? And now I'm respectably hidden from view, as are you, so who could possibly raise an objection if they found us companionably swimming together?"

HENRY COULDN'T KEEP his eyes off her. She was speaking to him, while undressing, as if she had not an inhibition in the world. It was only when she was about to remove her chemise that she indicated to him to turn his head.

When he heard her enter the water and then felt the gentle undulation of the waves, she made as she waded into chest height, announcing that she was now not indecent and they could resume proper conversation, he didn't know whether this was an invitation to something highly illicit.

But her manner seemed devoid of calculation and there was no subtext he could discern as she smiled at him, telling him about the dreary morning she'd had closeted with the other young ladies.

Finally, he had to stop her. "Miss Manners, is this normal behaviour in your part of the country? Swimming in summer with… members of the opposite sex?"

She stopped, surprised by his question, for she frowned and asked, "You've not seen so much as my ankles, have you, Mr Garrick? I'm not so beyond the pale that I don't know what a lady shows and what she doesn't. Besides, no one knows we're here and we can return to the house separately, and quite dry, and no one *will* know. I'm not going to tell them."

"And I certainly won't, either." He still couldn't fathom the strangeness of her behaviour, however, he would not look a gift horse in the mouth. If Miss Manners was happy to swim naked in his presence, he would not object. "Where did you say you hail from?" he asked.

"Dover. It's generally colder than here, however, it's not frowned upon to jump into the river when so inclined." She looked a trifle defensive. "That is, I didn't think it was. But then, I'm an orphan. A poor relation. Maybe I don't know as much as I thought about what was acceptable and what was not."

He put out his hand as she appeared distressed, and she looked grateful as she took it for a brief moment. "If you think I should not be here, then perhaps you'd be so good as to turn your head away again and I'll leave."

He didn't like that idea and wished he'd not said anything earlier to indicate his surprise at her behaviour, which she took as censure.

And censure it would be if anyone else came upon them.

Indeed, Henry would be in just as much trouble as she. Though he didn't care to think about that.

"The path doesn't naturally arrive at this part of the river and we are very distant from the grounds. I think we'll be safe enough," he said. He wanted to learn more of her strange upbringing. "I know only that you are here in place of your cousin, whom I've heard briefly mentioned. However, I am much more interested in you." He sent her a look that he hoped would invite her to share.

"We are a family of women." She held out her arms and seemed to study the sheen of water, without consciousness of his own admiration. "My older sisters have guided me."

"And are they married?"

Only now did she jerk up her head while he thought he detected evasiveness in her tone when she replied, "My sisters are not conventional. Neither has any wish to marry."

He could not hide his surprise. "So, they are independent women of independent means? While you are here in your cousin's stead for the... pleasure of it, Miss Manners? Are you like your sisters, or are you the black sheep of the family and wish for a ring upon your finger, despite your earlier assertions?" It was ungentlemanly perhaps to adopt this cynical tone but as he could also be more probing in the circumstances, he went on, "As the lowly dancing tutor, is it presumptuous of me to ask if you suspect you've been invited to Quamby House as a prospective wife for one of the young gentlemen Lady Quamby has invited?"

Miss Manners gave a gurgle of laughter, raising her eyes to the sky, her slender throat suddenly an object of intense fascination to Henry, who flicked his eyes to hers rather than succumbing to the pull of exploring that line downwards.

"I really could not say, Mr Garrick. I certainly am not in the same league as these other young ladies, so I would be highly surprised if Lady Quamby considered me a prospective match for any young gentlemen here. I had not considered that these few days of education were in fact a matchmaking venture by third parties who have prevailed upon the countess. My cousin did not think so, either, else I can't imagine she'd have suggested I go in her stead." She hesitated. "My cousin has a nicety of manner and connections far better than mine. No, Mr Garrick, I do not aspire to marriage with anyone here, so would much rather consort with you, even, than the young ladies who seem to regard me as..." She shrugged, looking for a word.

"More confident than the usual debutante?"

"More bold, I was going to say, and then didn't wish to tarnish myself in your eyes more than I already have."

He liked the way she said that. As if she really didn't care if she had or had not, for her expression was full of humour; and suddenly Henry felt the impulse to launch towards her and whisk her into his arms in the name of spontaneous teasing. Like he might have done with his cousin, Anna, a hoyden if ever there was one, who loved bouncing and splashing and who, he feared, was going to have a very miserable time when she came out in a few months' time.

"You're not the slightest bit tarnished in my eyes," he said, looking her over with an appreciation that made her blush.

"Then I fear I have given you the wrong impression, Mr Garrick." Embarrassment crossed her features. With a shrug and a laugh, she added, "Oh well, what does it signify if I don't wish to court your regard? I shall be here only a few days and when I'm gone, you'll hardly dwell on that pert miss who behaved with such cavalier lack of regard for the proprieties."

He hadn't realised he was so close to her until a movement with her hands caught his shoulder as she arced them out of the water to illustrate her words.

At the same time he'd moved his forearm and in the process her hand was suddenly skimming his palm, which he closed in a sudden reflex, causing her to pause, and stare.

But she didn't move her hand.

She moved nothing, as she remained rooted to the spot, still and unmoving, as he brought his other hand round to clasp her elbow.

For a long second they stared at one another, and Henry felt a voracious surge of desire through every extremity.

And might have acted upon it had the sounds of childish laughter not disturbed them, before three mud-spattered young boys suddenly appeared on the river's edge.

"You're swimming in our spot!" the dark-haired boy cried, indignant, before the other two brought up the rear. Their looks were much more interested, but Henry tried to assert a sense of normality as he called back, "It's our spot if we're already here, wouldn't you agree, boys?" he added, scooping up a handful of water.

Only to find Miss Manners had inadvertently moved in front of him and that the water he'd intended for the boys had caught her full in the face.

With a cry of shocked surprise, she plunged both her hands into the water and launched her own cascade in his direction, laughing as she realised, perhaps, the foolishness of her spontaneity.

Henry didn't mind. The tension was gone, and he was no longer the dangerously aroused young man who must remember himself.

Instead, he was the playful cousin, enjoying a water fight as he often had done with Anna.

The water sprayed all about them, their attempts to half drown the other became more contrived, until suddenly Miss Manners' lithe girlish body was wrapped about his as she gripped him round the throat as she might have done to her own brother.

Except that a brother would have responded with fraternal indignation.

Henry, by contrast, was struck by the most unbrotherly of emotions, his arms wrapping themselves about her chest, pinioning her against him.

She'd stopped the boisterous play, too. Now pliant, her body pressed against his, he heard the catch in her breath; saw the widening of her eyes.

"We're coming in, too!"

With a splash, the young boys had slithered down the water's edge and were now clinging to an overhanging tree branch as they began their own play. They seemed to have lost interest in the adults.

While Henry was acutely conscious of every faint breath—his and hers—and every point of contact: his hand upon the flare of her hip, the tip of her breast touching his chest, his other hand clasped in hers.

The turmoil in his loins.

"We should return to the house," he murmured, and she agreed; drawing away from him, taking a deep breath, flashing him a smile, then breaking past with present as she clapped her hands like a schoolmarm, exhorting the boys to look at the sky while she pulled herself out of the river's murky brown depths and then bent, reaching for her shawl.

She'd not told Henry he couldn't look.

His eyes followed the curve of her body as she sank down upon the leaves, covering herself with her shawl.

She didn't even glance at Henry. Her thoughts seemed on quite another plane as she slowly and methodically went through the motions of drying herself before pulling her chemise over her head, and then her clothes.

Henry didn't think he'd ever seen such graceful movements.

He didn't think he'd been so fascinated by a woman, either.

CHAPTER 5

From the drawing room window, Antoinette, Lady Quamby, watched the distant figure of Miss Manners make her way across the lawn, head bent as if deep in thought, her movements unhurried.

She was alone, and Antoinette wondered if she was feeling ostracised by the other young ladies. In fact, she was about to elicit her sister's thoughts on the matter when, turning, she found herself looking up at Mr Fortescue, whose own interested gaze was focussed upon Miss Manners.

"She's rather different from the usual crop of debs, eh?" he remarked, raising an eyebrow, his lips curved in an appreciative smile.

Mr Fortescue was older than the two blushing schoolboys who were the sons of acquaintances there to make up numbers, whereas, of course, Mr Garrick was Antoinette's real reason for this house party.

She needed to find him a wife, and she'd decided already that the most likely contender was elegant Miss Laidlaw. Not only did that young lady possess the right breeding, dowry, and other credentials, but Antoinette hadn't missed the interest in that young lady's eyes every time she rested them upon Henry.

But only when he wasn't looking.

And why wouldn't she be interested? With his charming manner and handsome address, the young man was a heartbreaker. But, of course, Miss Laidlaw would know she could not afford to lose her heart to him.

Mr Fortescue, by contrast, was the kind of gentleman a young lady like Miss Laidlaw would focus her attention upon.

And indeed, in public, she appeared interested and obliging whenever Mr Fortescue asked her to dance or addressed a remark to her. However—and this was where Antoinette excelled, she knew—there was no one like Antoinette who could sniff out a genuine romance.

Miss Laidlaw and darling Henry were going to make a match, she had already decided. Now all Antoinette had to do was ensure they had plenty of opportunities to be together so that they could establish an acquaintanceship that would be fanned by the fires of desire once Henry revealed himself in London as the new Lord Lomax in three weeks.

"Very different from the other young ladies, Mr Fortescue," Antoinette agreed. "And not aptly named," she added playfully. "There is a somewhat hoydenish air about her, and I'm sure she is quite different from her cousin Matilda, whom I had invited. Indeed, I'm not sure I would have permitted her to come in Matilda's stead had I known the other young ladies would take against her, so. For her own happiness," she added, not wishing to appear waspish.

She narrowed her eyes as the girl drew closer to the house. Clearly, Miss Manners was unaware of the scrutiny heaped upon her by the two pairs of eyes watching from the drawing room window. Her poke bonnet concealed most of her head, but now Antoinette saw that a long lock of her lustrous dark hair had escaped from the back of her coiffure, which was decidedly odd unless she'd removed her bonnet and engaged in some energetic outdoor activity.

And then, in the far distance, Antoinette spied Henry emerging from the vicinity of the river. He walked purposefully, raking back his hair with one hand as he raised his face to the sun.

What a handsome young man he was, Antoinette thought with a stab of fondness that overlaid her spasm of concern. For a moment, she'd wondered if they'd issued from a similar place. But then, she considered, Miss Manners was not the kind of young lady to attract Henry's interest when he had voiced a particular desire to ally himself with a respectable young lady of breeding who would slip easily into the role required of her.

Miss Manners was clearly a poor relation.

Mr Fortescue shifted beside her, drawing her attention as he murmured, "And, as such, quite fascinating, I think."

Antoinette studied him. Here was another gentleman in the market for a wife, but the way he was regarding Miss Manners was not at all how a gentleman regarded a wife.

"I'm sorry that I cannot provide you with more of Miss Manners' background," said Antoinette. "If I'd had fair warning I would have looked more deeply into it."

Mr Fortescue sent her a wolfish grin. "No need to apologise, Lady Quamby. I am quite happy to find out all I need to know myself."

His interest provided the overlay of relief that Antoinette needed following her momentary concern over the possibility that Henry and Miss Manners had been inadvertently thrown together in a situation that might promote a mutual regard.

She nodded at him. "An interest in Miss Manners at this evening's dance practice might ameliorate the angst she perhaps feels on account of the other young ladies forming a friendship that appears to exclude our young guest. Thank you, Mr Fortescue."

HOW DIFFERENT TILLY felt from the previous night. Then, she'd donned her beautiful ballgown loaned to her by Matilda with a certain defiance for the young ladies had been less than warm and welcoming earlier in the day. This had progressed to something close to hostility, with Miss Laidlaw's friend glancing at her askance and whispering loudly, "Definitely last season," as she'd passed Tilly in the corridor.

Now, as Tilly regarded that same ballgown in the privacy of her sumptuous bedchamber, she wondered how something so beautiful could garner such a reaction. What did it matter if it was this season, last season, or five seasons ago? Tilly had never worn anything so beautiful in all her life, the pale blue netting complementing her dark hair, which was now woven through with pearls.

Besides, it was only a dress. What really should count was the girl wearing it.

Yet even her sisters had regarded this week of Graceful Instruction, and the new gowns, as an opportunity not to be squandered.

Yasmin, the eldest, had narrowed her doe-brown eyes with their thick brows and asked, when Tilly had shown it to her, "How do you intend to profit from looking like a proper lady, Tilly my love? You are in for rich pickings, indeed."

"Well, I'm not going to steal anything, if that's what you're suggesting." Tilly had been indignant. "But I would like to see how these people live and perhaps make connections that could be valuable to all of us. That's worth more than if I were caught stealing."

Tilly always felt a little nervous when Yasmin said things like this. Yasmin was a woman of strong opinions and stronger appetites. She took what she wanted— baubles and trinkets she thought no one would miss, or that they might believe they'd misplaced; as well as lovers who quickly bored her.

Yasmin, though only thirteen years older, was also the mother Tilly had never had. Together with sister Zena, the pair had cared for Tilly as if she were a blood relative. They'd fed, clothed and comforted her.

But they were also keen to profit by her. After all, they lived a hand-to-mouth existence, though Tilly's gifts and therefore popularity with the better resourced ladies of the area, had led to opportunities.

Like this one, which Yasmin had been keen to see Tilly exploit.

Now, as Tilly descended the stairs, head bent and fortifying herself for the disparagement of the other young ladies who would, no doubt, be wearing new ballgowns, she was pleasantly aroused by a low noise of admiration from—as she looked up— the young dancing master.

"I have been given a second chance to tell you how much your gown becomes you," he said, approaching from an oppo- site corridor.

"According to Miss Laidlaw, it's two seasons old, and I most certainly should be ashamed of wearing it a second time," Tilly said, putting her hand demurely to her locket before reverently running her forefinger over the embroidery at her breast.

"Well, I'd not have known it was two seasons old, and I'm sure most gentlemen wouldn't have, either," he went on, showing no inclination to move on and confirming, by the look in his eyes, that their encounter earlier in the day was not an aberration based purely on the fact that she'd showed more boldness than Tilly suspected a young lady in her position ought to have shown.

Tilly drew in a breath and wondered if this is what it felt like to wear tight stays, for she really couldn't quite get the air she needed. The smile Mr Garrick was levelling at her made her knees feel wobbly and her head a little light.

But she recovered quickly and said, "Then your words have given me the confidence to enjoy this evening."

"How could you *not* enjoy the evening when Lady Quamby and her sister have laid on such novel entertainment?"

Tilly considered this. "It is not pleasant to be judged by one's fellow debutantes and found wanting."

"Well, I certainly don't find you wanting, and shall be happy to lead you onto the dance floor to demonstrate our steps. You are a gifted dancer and a quick learner, and if your gown is two years old, then the fashions today are not nearly as becoming."

"What a very nice little speech, Mr Garrick," Tilly said, fluttering her eyelashes. "My head is quite turned. Ah, and here are the young ladies hailing you, so I shall withdraw if I am not to suffer their displeasure."

She liked the flare of disappointment he didn't trouble to hide.

But she liked, even more, that he held true to his promise later that evening. Not only did she enjoy the jolt of feeling that coursed through her when Mr Garrick took her hand and rested his other briefly on the small of her back; she enjoyed, too, the flare of displeasure in Miss Laidlaw's eyes before that young lady smiled up at Mr Fortescue and allowed him to lead her onto the dance floor, instead.

This latter gentleman was of course far more a match for Miss Laidlaw who wanted only the admiration of Mr Garrick to bolster her opinion of herself, Tilly thought; which gave her a sense of relief.

No, Tilly and the dancing tutor were far better matched than Miss Laidlaw and Mr Garrick. And Mr Garrick would know it well.

In fact, as the evening wore on, he did not trouble to hide his interest in Tilly, as his eyes followed her about the room, even though he was assiduous in his attention to the young ladies he'd been engaged to tutor.

Surprisingly, Mr Fortescue also made clear his interest in Tilly. He was quick to engage her for the second dance doing a swap with Mr Garrick and transferring his pouting dancing partner, Miss Laidlaw, into his arms.

Though Tilly noticed the pout was only for show for that young lady quickly became animated as she expounded upon whatever it was that ladies of breeding and a modicum of education expounded upon.

Tilly had found that the only topics over which she could wax lyrical were herb treatments, possets and healing properties of certain plants, and how to create pleasing hair styles; subjects that would hardly interest either Mr Fortescue or Mr Garrick.

So, she was surprised when, once again in the arms of Mr Garrick, he said, "Now, you were telling me a fascinating anecdote about the use of spider webs in healing wounds. Where did you learn of such things? Certainly not in the schoolroom."

"Oh, I was never in the schoolroom," Tilly said blithely before pressing her lips together as she remembered that the young lady she was emulating would most certainly have spent most of her days closeted in a spartan, airless chamber, like Matilda, with a governess.

"As I might have told you," she began in the spirit of confession, "my upbringing was hardly conventional and my… cousin, Matilda… and her side of the family look down upon our branch as quite beyond redemption."

"Yet you seem to have learned a great many matters of more relevance to life than the rest of these young ladies who are here only to find themselves a position among the titled."

Tilly shrugged. "Where I live, I am called upon to help with healing amongst those who have lost faith in the doctor, though I am not as gifted as my sister, who is regarded as a weaver of miracles by some." Tilly was proud to say it. Had he guessed who and what she was? He must surely be coming to some understanding of the fact that Tilly was an imposter, or at least, certainly not a young lady of the ton. Yet that didn't seem to put him off, and why should it? A dancing master and a young woman of Tilly's abilities and experience would make a fine match as they travelled the country in furtherance of Mr Garrick's profession.

She caught herself up. What kind of daydreaming was this? Tilly had never imagined herself living anywhere other than in the cottage she shared with her two sisters. Yasmin was always the first to remind them that those who lived in houses such as Quamby House were to be pitied and that their own simple, hand-to-mouth existence was far nobler.

Though, now she thought about it, it wasn't true that she'd dismissed any idea of leaving her home with her sisters.

That dashing, confidence-stealing reprobate she'd met at the hiring fair two years before had led her to believe he wanted to whisk her away as his own.

And she'd liked the idea. Even if he was only a groom. Or a footman. With his muscular build and broad shoulders, he could have been either.

But now Tilly was here, basking in the admiration of a man she recognised, with the benefit of experience and maturity, offered her a much better future. And, furthermore, she'd bet on the fact that Henry Garrick was as honest and reliable as her first lover was not.

A light supper was provided when the dancing was finished and Tilly found herself alone for the first time this evening and, to her dismay, regarding Miss Laidlaw with distinct jealousy as that young lady commandeered Mr Garrick's attention.

"May I help you refill your plate, Miss Manners?" It was Mr Fortescue, offering her his arm to lead her back to the table. She didn't want to go, but nor did she wish to be rude.

"Alas, the excitement of today has been too great for one who has lived so long secluded," Tilly said, politely disengaging her hand and stepping away. "If you'll excuse me, I think I shall retire for the night."

"Do you know how to navigate this great house, Miss Manners? You may get lost between here and the Long Gallery. Pray, allow me to accompany you at least to the wing in which you're accommodated."

Tilly shook her head. "Thank you, but no, Mr Fortescue," she said firmly but with a smile, not looking at the rest of the company before she took herself off, following a cursory thank you to her hostess.

She was sorry not to have had the chance to say goodnight to Mr Garrick but she could hardly draw attention to herself and the feelings she had for him and, besides, Miss Laidlaw was in an animated discussion about some astonishing sight she'd beheld at the Tower of London.

Tilly had never felt in such disordered spirits as she navigated her way from the ballroom to the main staircase before choosing the corridor that led to her bedchamber via the Long Gallery.

This was a room to lose herself in, all on its own, she thought, gazing at the suits of sixteenth century armour, the massive tapestries and the plaster busts and other antiquities from around the world.

What would Yasmin think of this? she wondered. Her scornful sister would no doubt have something derisive to say, which sent a stab of guilt through Tilly for, in fact, feeling a certain reverence as she stroked the polished metal plates once worn by some noble Tudor warrior.

"You look as if you're about to give him your colours," she heard a voice say, and her heart leapt to see Mr Garrick advancing towards her, a look of intent upon his handsome features as he added, "You know the ladies bestowed their favours in the form of coloured scarves upon the jousters. I daresay it's the least they could do since the poor fellow might well be embarking upon his last hour on this mortal coil. Would you bestow your colours upon me?"

"My colours and my favours, Mr Garrick," Tilly said, archly, knowing this was the very right thing to say, and also the perfect prelude to being swept up into his arms and his kiss – passionate, and with no preliminaries, just as she knew would happen from the moment they'd inadvertently touched each other in the water earlier that day.

She'd barely finished the thought before she was in his embrace and his lips were upon hers, passionate and demanding.

When they broke apart, it was without embarrassment but with an intense throbbing of desire. She knew he felt as she as he cupped her face and looked into her eyes, his breath fast and faint.

Her own grasp on present reality seemed suddenly disordered, and her knees weak and unsteady. She was glad she had Mr Garrick's strong, muscular body for support in a way that was far more satisfying that when he held her on the dance floor.

Just as he opened his mouth to speak—or to kiss her again—approaching voices echoed through the corridor. Quickly, Mr Garrick put his hands on her shoulders and steered her into the shadows behind a large screen.

It was Miss Laidlaw and her two friends, chattering and laughing as they went by, their words indistinct save for the derisive "...two seasons old..."

Damning, hurtful words, except that as Tilly jerked up her head in indignation, she encountered first Mr Garrick's smiling eyes and then his wonderfully impassioned lips meeting hers in a kiss, more considered and with more finesse, though just as wonderful, as their first.

CHAPTER 6

THE NEXT MORNING PASSED IN A BLUR. TILLY FELT SHE WAS
walking on air as she partook of breakfast, yearning for an
absent Mr Garrick, before being visited by the most tumul-
tuous, torturous of sensations when there he was, in the ballroom, his eyes brightening at the sight of her; though he
managed the necessary restraint as he greeted the other young
ladies, and Mr Fortescue, and the gangly youths whose names
she could not remember.

Now it was easy to remain quiet and pliant in the background, as Miss Laidlaw made a coy remark at some quip
issued by the clever dancing master. Mr Garrick was, Tilly
could see, becoming more of an object of interest on the behalf
of the young ladies. Even though they would never consider
him husband material, as he would need to make his own way
in the world, he was handsome, affable, and surprisingly
cultured.

Just the kind of husband that Tilly was seeking.

The fizzing exhilaration she felt at his touch was mutual.
They were meant for each other, destinies entwined. Yasmin
claimed she'd seen it in her crystal ball, cross that Tilly hadn't

taken seriously her prognostication that Tilly's week away would secure her future with the man of her dreams.

"You'd be so much happier if you if you could take lovers as it pleases Zena and myself, and not be beholden to one man," she'd said with a sigh. "Marriage!" She's spat the word.

Tilly was not one to dwell on past mistakes. Everyone made them, which was why the future always held such exciting possibilities.

Like Mr Garrick.

Snippets of his conversation with her host and hostess, Lord and Lady Quamby, revealed him to be surprisingly informed on world matters.

Yet he was merely a dancing tutor. He needed to travel to earn his living, and Tilly would make the ideal helpmate with her gift for healing through her knowledge of the medicinal properties of herbs and plants. Together, they would be eagerly sought after as a duo of talent and usefulness.

When a picnic was proposed, Tilly turned quickly to see Mr Garrick seeking her out. She was surprised at the look in his eyes and the brief, secretive shaking of his head, but she took her cue from him and, despite her initial enthusiasm for the idea, cried off due to a megrim.

As did Mr Garrick, who had other matters to which he had to attend.

Clearly, this was a disappointment to certain young ladies in the party who had eagerly endorsed the idea in its development. But when the note arrived in Tilly's room as she supposedly rested, she saw the merit in ensuring everyone but themselves was safely distant.

"Meet me at the river as soon as you can get away."

It was brief and made no bones about Mr Garrick's desire to be alone with her once more.

Tilly donned walking boots, bonnet and shawl and, as soon as she saw the carriage bearing the three young ladies, and three gentlemen, together with Lady Quamby, rolling through the gates, she slipped out through the kitchen courtyard and wove her way over the hill behind the house, veering round to meet the river, well out of sight of anyone, she hoped.

He was already there, standing by a large gnarled tree root, striding forwards to take her in his arms in a spontaneous burst of delighted passion that sent her mind spinning.

When they broke away, he took her hand in his and together they began to negotiate the uneven path.

"Did I meet you only two days ago?" he asked in wonder. "I feel like I've known you my whole lifetime."

Tilly nodded. She felt the same. "I could never have imagined this when I came here."

He stopped and turned, taking both her hands in his. "What *were* your expectations when you came here?" He hesitated. "You would not get a London season, I gather. Had you hoped to meet some eligible gentlemen? Men with titles and pocket-books like Mr Fortescue?"

Tilly shook her head. "No, Mr Garrick—"

"Henry," he interrupted. "If I may call you Tilly?"

"Of course. I think we are definitely on Christian name terms," she agreed.

"Tilly, I like it." He smiled. "Was the diminutive on account of your cousin being called Matilda?

She frowned. *What was he talking about?*

"Matilda is the name written on the back of your brooch." He touched the brooch pinned to her shawl, carved and painted as a rose. "I noticed it when we were… bathing in the river." He raised an eyebrow and she giggled.

"Yes. My cousin… Matilda… wanted to remain at her home due to a certain visitor being in the neighbourhood. I, on the other hand, wanted to enjoy a different environment, in a grand house, wearing the borrowed wardrobe that my cousin pressed upon me if I would go in her. I think she'd not have approved of my bathing in the river."

"I think she'd not have approved of me showing you such interest. Are you disappointed that I have seized the advantage ahead of those other, far more eligible gentlemen?"

Tilly shook her head fiercely. "Not at all. Oh Henry, I've never felt this feeling before." She touched her heart, and he drew her against his chest, tucking her head beneath his chin as she went on. "I liked you so much more than *any* of those other gentlemen the moment I saw your smile and heard your kind words to Miss Dorley when she stumbled, rather than making her feel as clumsy as she is."

"Then I am flattered and honoured. To think that a young lady who could have her pick of eligible gentlemen, if only you were granted a season in London, should have preferred me."

Tilly dropped her gaze. "I am not a catch like my cousin Matilda. But," she looked at him shyly, "let's not talk of that and squander the time alone we have together."

"Indeed!" He snatched up her hand, and they began to walk, meandering by the river, enjoying the warmth of the sun, though dark grey clouds were scudding across the sky.

"We must make sure they do not discover us when the others return in the carriage," said Tilly, aware that they'd rejoined the road. "Let's take that path over the hill. I'm sure we can cross the land of the manor house without being caught trespassing."

"You're right. And in any case, the manor house is unoccupied until the winter, I'm told."

By the time they had reached the sand coloured building, the clouds had darkened and a light spattering of rain had them lengthening their stride.

They stopped beneath the portico to get their breath, scanning the hillside as they stood, side by side at the top of the steps.

"Do you know who lived here?" Tilly asked. "It's very grand." She wished she hadn't said that. It made her sound provincial, but he was smiling when she glanced up to see him studying her.

"It's a nice house, but your cousin must live in something just as large and comfortable, for it's hardly a grand country estate."

"I'm sure you're used to working in many of those," Tilly said, deflecting the subject so she'd not be forced to answer. Miss Matilda did indeed live in a house finer than this, but she'd rather not have to evade the truth any more than she necessary.

"It's true that I'm used to grand homes and would find it difficult to adapt to a homely cottage as an impecunious dancing master." His mouth quirked. "Would you think as much of me if I lived in a humble dwelling… like that one?" He pointed to a small thatched cottage in the distance, overrun by rambling roses. Tilly thought it looked sweet and inviting. Compared with her own cramped living quarters, which she shared with her two sisters, the thatched cottage *was* like a grand country estate.

"Where you live has nothing to do with what I feel about you, Henry." She put her hand on his sleeve. "Why don't we look inside? I can see a half-open window in the basement."

With a laugh, first of pleasure at her words, then at her boldness, he snatched up her hand and together they ran down the front steps, leading her to the servants' downstairs entrance. It was locked, but a nearby casement window was open a few inches.

"It is raining, after all," he said, by way of justification, "and you and I both look respectable enough that we won't be marched off to the magistrate for trespassing if someone comes upon us."

Tilly had no difficulty in climbing through the window, assisted by Henry, who whisked her into his arms on the other side and swung her round before setting her down on the dusty floorboards.

"No one has been here for a while, by the look of it," he observed, pointing to the marks made by their feet in the overlay of dust. "We have the run of the place. Come, let's explore."

Tilly was just as eager. She might have done so alone, but it was so much more enjoyable with company. Especially the company of her handsome Henry, who kept hold of her hand as together they wove through the rooms and corridors of the elegant, commodious country house.

Dust sheets covered the furniture and in a bedchamber with blue flock wallpaper, they stopped by the window, raising a blind to look out into the dreary weather. The blue skies that had smiled upon them when they'd stepped out for their walk were a low, thick grey.

"It'll be awhile before it clears," Tilly said. "But I suppose a little rain never hurt anyone."

Henry lounged against the window still and regarded her with a considered smile. "I'd like to see you at the end of a rain-soaked walk, but I'd rather while away the time waiting for the weather to improve by kissing you. What do you say to that, Tilly, my love?"

The combination of lustful intent, admiration, and the endearment was potent. Tilly felt her mouth stretch in a happy, colluding smile, not ashamed that she was so eager and transparent. She'd heard Matilda say often enough how important it was to lure a gentleman by not appearing too eager. Gentlemen like the good chase, Matilda had quoted.

But Henry had already made his admiration clear. The two of them were head over heels with each other. She believed that with confidence. They'd passed the stage of navigating whatever courtly ritual fine ladies felt necessary to their dignity – or the dignity of the gentleman. She wasn't sure which it was, just as she wasn't sure of any of the strange guidelines by which the gentry lived.

"Who will make the first move?" she asked, pertly.

He took a step forward, arms outstretched, obviously expecting her to step into his embrace, for he closed his eyes, only to blink them open in surprise when he saw she'd stepped backwards, towards the door. For a moment, he looked a trifle uncertain until Tilly laughed.

"I've made it much too easy for you, Mr Garrick, when I really am not that kind of young lady. You can kiss me if you can catch me." Picking up her skirts, she dashed into the corridor, laughing to hear his footsteps right behind her.

Tilly was fleet of foot. She'd spent her childhood dashing about the woods, on occasion chasing what they hoped to eat that night, or just out of youthful high spirits with the other ragged children who sometimes joined them.

At the entrance to one of the bedrooms, he clearly thought he had her cornered when he blocked the doorway, then came round the bed. But with a squeal, she leapt onto and over the bed, dashing through the doorway with a last glimpse of Henry, who looked quite taken aback.

Good, he needed to know what she was truly like. Not some buttoned-up miss, like the other debutantes at Lady Quamby's. It might embolden him more, besides, for he'd be concerned at the social divide. However confident the young dancing master really was, he'd still baulk at the idea that the young lady with whom he wished to ally himself was as elevated as he clearly thought her.

"I thought you liked being kissed!" he called after her, and Tilly, pausing to look over her shoulder before she darted into another bedroom, this time decorated in tones of crimson and gold, said, "Only by you! But we appreciate best what we've worked hard for."

He laughed as he stood in the doorway of the red chamber

and sized her up. Tilly stood by the window, ready to dart past him when he advanced.

Only this time he anticipated her next move, as well as her athleticism, lunging onto the bed to grab her ankle as she tried to cross the mattress.

"Victory!" he growled, rolling on top of her and, without preliminary, bringing his mouth down to hers.

Her struggle was minimal. In fact, Tilly only wriggled beneath him so he wasn't crushing her breast and so she could kiss him back in comfort and without restriction.

She liked the weight of him. The kissing was highly arousing, but the evidence of his own excitement as his sharp angles pressed into her belly was even more so.

The long-latent desire for a man surged through her body and flooded her lower belly, and she heard her soft sigh become a faint moan of longing.

"Henry, you kiss so… divinely," she whispered, running the tip of her tongue over his top lip before plundering the seam of his lips and plunging it into his mouth in a fierce escalation of passion.

She felt his increasing ardour and then his effort at reining in his passion.

But why should he stop? Did he really have to play the gentleman when Tilly was just as needy as he?

With a push, she wriggled out from beneath him and he clearly thought she was putting a stop to matters, for she saw surrender and faint embarrassment on his face, before Tilly rolled on top of him. "Now you're my prisoner," she said with a laugh as she straddled him, gazing down into his face as she adopted an expression of playful intent.

He looked about to protest for a shadow crossed his face. But then Tilly's mouth was upon his, and her hands were exploring his body; caressing his face, contouring the ridges of his chest then, further down, over his tight stomach.

He kissed her back with enthusiasm, but gripped her wrist when her hand strayed over the front of his breeches, shaking his head; while she gripped his thighs within her own, the urgency to feel as one with him powering through her loins.

"No, Tilly, don't—" He ground out raggedly between kisses.

"Don't you want me?" she asked. For what man who professed to be in love objected to consummating those feelings? It was the most natural consequence of desire in the world.

"Of course I do. But you're an innocent—"

"Not so innocent." She shook her head. "I know what to do and how to take care. Henry? Please say yes…" The look in his eyes was gratifying, for there was both surrender and a flare of surprised excitement at her words.

Tilly didn't waste time. She closed her eyes and let his hands wander, sucking in a breath of pleasurable anticipation as he massaged the heated skin of her thighs while she fumbled with the buttons of his fly fall. Then she squealed as he flipped her onto her back once more and straddled her, his expression one of smouldering desire when she blinked.

"My darling, but I adore you," he growled, running his tongue over his top lip before he plundered her mouth once more, his hands roaming over her buttocks before finding the sweet spot between her legs.

"Ohhh," she breathed, the escalation of burning need making her clamp her knees tighter around his waist while she ran her hands up the thighs of his breeches before insinuating her hand into the gap where she felt him, hot and heavy and so ready for her.

"Oh, yes!" she whispered, her core pulsing with desire, her heart skittering about her chest like a trapped bird. It was both exciting and alarming, but mostly it was the most thrilling affirmation that she truly had found the man she wanted to spend her life with.

She was only going to give herself to one man. She'd made the pledge two years ago after her first experience with the man whom her sisters had encouraged her to lie with in what they believed was an essential and timely initiation.

And Tilly had enjoyed it.

At the time.

But he'd proved not to be the kind and enthusiastic youth she'd thought him. His ruthlessness and jealousy had sucked all sweetness from the memory of their brief two weeks of passion.

And Tilly had vowed that she'd never repeat the experience.

The next man she lay with would be the man who would become her husband.

CHAPTER 7

Tilly opened her eyes slowly as she snuggled into Henry's side. Smiling, she reached up her forefinger to stroke away the faint frown lines.

"That was… unexpected," he said, blinking. He looked as if he didn't know what else to say.

"I don't think it was." Tilly nibbled her lower lip before rolling over to nibble his. "We've been moving towards this since we were first introduced, don't you think? When you touched me in the water. Remember?"

A beatific smile crossed his face as he stared at the ceiling, his memories obviously happy ones.

"How could I forget? It's not every day a young lady is happy to bathe naked with a gentleman."

Henry's hand trailed over her side. For a long while he was silent and Tilly, basking in the closeness, was roused when he whispered, "You indicated this wasn't your first time. Have there been many others?"

"Of course not." She settled on her back, close to him, and stared at the ceiling. "My sisters were always quite insistent that

I must never marry without knowing what a lifetime of the marital bed would be like."

"The sisters who never wish to marry?"

Tilly raised herself on one elbow and gazed down at him. "I'm not like them."

He frowned as if trying to grasp her meaning. "What do you mean by that?" he asked finally. Tilly realised this conversation was difficult for him and suddenly was embarrassed.

"My sisters… enjoy men, but they don't want to be tied to one man for a lifetime."

"And how are you different?"

Tilly shrugged. "I want to find a man for a lifetime, but I don't want to take any chances—"

"You said you knew how to… take care of those things. Chances."

"I would not have a child out of wedlock, and I know enough about herbs and healing to be confident I won't. My sisters, however, care nothing for society's conventions. I was referring to the fact I won't take chances when it comes to who I intend to spend my life with."

"But you've been with men before?"

"Only one." Tilly registered his tenseness. Of course, she knew Miss Matilda lived by a different code of behaviour; behaviour that seemed silly and unrelated to Tilly when her friend had tried to explain them.

This week at Quamby House was supposed to provide the very education Tilly needed regarding how to behave like a lady. She'd certainly never expected to meet a man on the first day who she felt almost instantly was the very man to whom she wished to commit herself—in conventional marriage—for the rest of her life.

Henry's enjoyment up to this moment had been apparent. Tilly wondered why he wanted to dwell on something so unsatisfactory and that clearly had gone nowhere—such as her previous experience with a man—when they could be enjoying the present.

"Who was he?"

His voice was low, his tone difficult to interpret.

Still, Tilly wasn't going to lie. Henry knew she was not of the same social class as the other ladies here, so she might as well tell him everything else he wanted to know. "I met him at a fair. He was handsome and… attentive. My sisters thought we would suit." Tilly shrugged. "But we didn't."

"A fair?" Henry exclaimed, before apparently attempting to calm himself. "So… he left you…" He swallowed, cleared his voice and tried again. "He left you after he had taken what he wanted? Did he… hurt you?"

Tilly hesitated. This really did seem to trouble him more than it should, for there was a look of something raw and angry in his eye. Oh well, best to get this conversation over with. "He didn't hurt me but he wasn't a very good man," she replied. "However, he didn't take what I didn't offer. My body, I mean."

"Good lord, what are you saying, Tilly?"

Tilly shifted, then sat up. What was happening with their cosy lovemaking? This wonderful togetherness had seemed the culmination of everything she'd hoped it would be.

Until now.

She rose to kneel beside him, emotion threatening to get the better of her as she gripped the bed head and looked down at him. "I'm saying that I met a man and, as I thought I might like to marry him, my sisters encouraged us to be together. However, after several weeks, I realised he would be far from the kind and caring husband I was looking for and was very glad not to have been forced into a decision I would regret for the rest of my life. Are you condemning me for that? Would you not do the same?"

❄

THIS STOPPED Henry in his tracks. Would he not do the same? Play the field before he chose a suitable young woman to be his bride?

He wasn't sure how to respond, as he met the fierceness in her look. She was staring down at him, half upright against the headboard, her arms now crossed over her naked breasts. His eyes raked her lovely form: her smooth, shapely arms, the delicious undulation where her hips flared out from a small, neat waist. Everything below that was hidden, but he'd experienced their perfection.

"I am a man, Tilly," he said, finding it difficult to get out the words as he drew himself up to her level. "The rules are different." Quickly he went on when he saw her expression darken, "Men don't expect the women they take as their wives to have had… experience of other men."

To his surprise, she nodded slowly, as if considering this to have merit. "My sisters told me that this was the expectation amongst people of a certain class." She cleared her throat. "However, being a family of women, and not being of the gentry, they said we had the freedom to do things differently. To explore the way forward in a way that suited *us*, not the men who wanted us."

This shocked him. "Surely your cousin Matilda counselled you against… spoiling your chances—"

"Spoiling my chances?" She cut in sharply, her eyes blazing before she scrambled over the mattress and stood up. "I did not come to Lady Quamby's House Party to look for a husband. Meeting you, and discovering how much I liked you, was very unexpected. Nor am I going to London like Cousin Matilda, who was brought up with quite different expectations. I've never pretended to be anything other than I am but if my … *laxness* troubles you so much that you believe it implies a deficiency of moral character, then I am glad I followed my own way of… weeding out a man who I *thought* might suit me, as well as any other whose trivial concerns focus on finding a bride who was virtuous and obedient and would dance to their tune until the end of time."

He didn't want this, and her words touched a nerve. "Tilly, stay!"

But she shook her head as she smoothed out her skirts. Her long dark hair had come unbound but her deft fingers worked quickly to restore order while she went on, focused on her task, "I was instantly attracted to you, Mr Garrick, because apart from being obviously handsome, you also seemed kind and generous of spirit." Her voice was low and angry and she didn't look at him as she put herself to rights. "I thought I liked the way you looked at the world and I relished the chance to take things between us further so that I could indeed see if your vision and outlook on life accorded with mine." Drawing in a breath, she stopped to fix him with a fulminating look. "For, you see, I will not be made to feel a lesser mortal because of the way I choose to safeguard my heart, and perhaps my future. Fore-warned is forearmed, Mr Garrick." With a swish of her skirts, and a brittle display of magnificent dignity, she swung round and made for the door.

"Tilly, please come back. I didn't mean—"

She cut him off, turning. "I am not the kind of young lady you were looking for and so I will not waste more of your time, Mr Garrick. I did not give myself through idle dalliance, and it pains me that you think such a thing. But I don't suppose our motives matter, since it is my past behaviour that you find deplorable." She sniffed. "And I can't change that."

Henry didn't know what to say that would make her stay, but he had to try. "It doesn't change the way I feel about you." They were the first words he could think of, but understand-ably, she scoffed at them.

"Every word and action since we lay together makes it clear

it does. Good day, Mr Garrick. I know my way back to Quamby House."

He sat on the edge of the bed and let her go because his thoughts were too disordered to do otherwise. No, she was not the virtuous, uncomplicated virgin a man of his position needed to marry.

But he didn't think he could desire anyone more.

TILLY RETURNED TO QUAMBY HOUSE BY A CIRCUITOUS ROUTE so she could stop in a copse of trees away from the path and cry.

She didn't understand what had happened. Henry had judged her as wanting for doing the very thing he wanted.

It made no sense. This world of rarefied manners was not her world.

Nor had she thought it was Henry's world. Why was it so wrong to be with a man if she thought he might be the man with whom she wished to throw in her lot?

Except that, clearly, Henry hadn't been as serious as Tilly had regarding a future together.

The distant rumble of thunder added a further overlay to her dismal mood. Everything was bleak and grey in her life right now and the faint scratchings of the woodland creatures punctuating the quiet was an earthy reminder that her place was amidst the trees and countryside, cosy on her hard bed in the hovel she shared with her sisters; not lying between fine linen sheets in a fine house.

Eyes closed, she ran her palms down the tree trunk as she drew in another shuddering sob.

Shrieking as she felt a hand on her shoulder.

Then she was pulled into a tight, familiar embrace, Henry's cologne overlaid with sandalwood soap, his stubbled cheek grazing hers as he plundered her lips.

"Forgive me, Tilly," he ground out, squeezing her as if he couldn't get close enough. "My behaviour was unforgivable."

Tilly said nothing when it was enough to let her silence speak to her agreement, and her enthusiasm in meeting his kiss, answer to her feelings for him.

When their passion was spent, she rested her head against his chest and listened to his soft breathing. It was all the comfort she needed. Grand protestations of undying love were nothing compared to his simple attempts at atonement and his wish for her forgiveness.

"I'm a disappointment if you wanted a proper lady, Henry," she finally said, pressing her face against the rough fabric of his waistcoat.

"You are lady enough for me, Tilly," he replied. "Even if your behaviour is… unconventional. At least you're more honest than many young ladies with pretensions they cannot uphold."

"And you've got more character than many of the fine gentleman of my acquaintance," she told him, tilting her chin to look up at him. "Now, are you going to lead me into Lady Quamby's ball tomorrow night so I can make all the other young ladies jealous?"

"Jealous? Of the young lady dancing with the dancing master?" He smiled. "You are kind, my dear."

"I speak the truth. You are a mile ahead of the other gentlemen there." She was proud to declare it so, but again he scoffed gently as he tucked her hand into the crook of his arm and began to walk her back towards Quamby House.

"I am honoured that you put me ahead of dashing Mr Fortescue, whom I notice is not averse to taking you into the waltz when he can claim you first."

"Mr Fortescue is very dashing, I will allow," said Tilly with a prim, playful smile. "But he is also very aware of his great attraction for the ladies. You, my darling Henry, have an air of unconcern about you that is quite irresistible. All the young debutantes looking for husbands would swoon over you if you were not merely the dancing tutor, and I would not get a look in." She patted his hand, adding, "And that's just the way I like it."

They wandered the path in companionable silence before Henry asked, "And what else would make you happy, Miss Manners? If it were within my power to give it to you?"

"That's a very large and dangerous question, Mr Garrick. Why, your acceptance of me the way I am, I suppose." She looked ahead as they walked. She'd not expected the question and so hadn't thought upon the answer, but the words she spoke were the truth. "Do I have that?" She stopped to slant a look up at him. "Or is there an exacting mama in the wings who would take exception to behaviour that you've indicated is not within the accepted boundaries?"

"There is a mama who does have exacting standards, but as her love for her son outweighs everything else, I do not foresee difficulties."

A thrill of expectation coursed through Tilly. Lord, he was speaking as if there really might be a future between them.

"And what of you, Tilly? You have two sisters with unconventional thoughts on marriage. Would they thumb their nose at any suitor who knocks on your door? And what of your closest male relative? Every young lady has one of those, surely?"

"I don't," said Tilly, easily. "I have no male relatives and I never have."

"What about your cousin's guardian? Surely he exercises some authority?"

"Who?" Tilly asked before realising her lapse. "You mean Mr

Collins? Goodness, he's lax enough with regard to keeping Matilda properly maintained and disciplined. Like I said, I'm from the down-at-heel branch of the family. The rules that apply to Matilda do not apply to me." She hesitated. "There is more I could tell you that would shock you."

He hesitated. Then shrugged, which she took as an invitation to unburden herself of the worst.

"I had a third sister who had a child out of wedlock."

Yes, this did appear to shock him. In fact, shock seemed to have robbed him of speech.

"The father was a nobleman who refused responsibility after he'd promised her marriage. She lost her mind, gave the child away to the foundling home, and then—" She wasn't sure how to finish. "Then she died the next day."

"Oh, Tilly, I am so sorry." He seemed truly moved. "Perhaps that explains more about you than—"

She cut him off. "It explains nothing, for Becca lived by her own code, just as live by mine, which I have explained to you. We are a strange family and perhaps not one your mama would wish you to associate with."

Covertly, she watched him. She really had told him the worst that a young dancing tutor who lived a middling kind of existence could digest. His mama did not need to know everything, but as long as Henry did, matters could proceed with her conscience clear.

"Well, I look forward to meeting your family, strange though they sound." They'd reached a small hill where they stopped to overlook the sweeping countryside. "I may do that, surely? Call on you?"

Tilly smiled. "Of course you may. But, like I said, we are not well positioned like Matilda. I have no male relative and I have no dowry. In fact, I have nothing to my name, so I'm not sure that you would in fact wish to call on me."

He brought up her hand and kissed the knuckles. "I am

looking for a woman with a sunny disposition, a lively sense of humour, and an enthusiasm for life to match mine." He stared into her eyes a moment. "Whether or not she has what my mama might consider a suitable background, or a dowry is immaterial to me."

CHAPTER 9

clasped in his."

Tilly thought Henry's voice sounded adorably authoritative as Lady Fenton accompanied the instructions with a few bars on the keyboard.

She was partnering Mr Fortescue, whose hand upon her waist was just a little too close and proprietorial. She flashed a look at Henry, who was partnering Miss Laidlaw, and he raised one eyebrow; but in so subtle a manner that no one would have noticed.

This was how they'd agreed to play it.

"I might lose my position if it became known that the mere dancing tutor had designs upon one of the precious debutantes in Lady Quamby's care," he'd said.

After they'd made love the second time.

Tilly had burst out laughing. She was hardly the precious debutante he thought her.

He'd joined her in mocking the statement.

Perhaps she'd revealed too much about the reality of her situation, but how much worse it would have been if he'd been too afraid to touch her in the mistaken belief that she was socially so much above him.

"Now, ladies, left foot back, right foot, back—"

Mr Fortescue was an excellent dancer, she had to give him that. He knew how to lead, he was decisive, pleasant in his conversation; guiding her and entertaining her while he did it.

But he was no substitute for Henry. Not her darling Henry, who was just a menial in a grand household but who seemed to exert an authority equal to Mr Fortescue's while everything else about him was so much more appealing.

Let Miss Laidlaw initiate a swap when the music ended. She was clearly intent upon seeking a man who would satisfy her matrimonial aspirations.

After she'd satisfied her desire to flirt with a handsome man.

The knowledge was comforting to Tilly. Miss Laidlaw was no threat, even if it was clear how much she fancied Henry. For, clearly, Miss Laidlaw would not marry a mere dancing tutor.

"Wonderful!" Lady Quamby clapped her hands when the last notes faded away, and the young people milled about the dancing floor, most looking flushed and awkward, while Henry conversed with his employer and Mr Fortescue stepped closer to Tilly to say, "You dance divinely, Miss Manners. I look forward to repeating the experience in London in a couple of weeks. You will, of course, be resident in the capital for the season?"

Tilly sighed. "Alas, I will not, Mr Fortescue."

He looked surprised, as Tilly supposed he would, since every young lady's objective here was to marry. And, as young people of a certain standing, the precursor would, of course, include several months in London as part of their come-out.

He gripped her forearm impulsively and whispered, just as Lady Quamby reclaimed everyone's attention, "A great can happen between then and now to change *that*, Miss Manners.

AND NOW WAS the evening that Henry's unlikely benefactress, Lady Quamby, had planned as the culmination of her little gathering: The culmination of her noble experiment to find Henry a wife who would love him for himself rather than what he offered.

Unexpectedly, Henry had found her. And found that his fascination for her was based on where he'd least expected a young lady would wield power over him.

With her originality.

Yes, her refreshing originality.

In the yellow drawing room, Ladies Quamby and Fenton lounged on the Egyptian sofa, chatting amiably together while their husbands leaned against the mantelpiece, discussing horseflesh in between gusty intakes of snuff on Lord Quamby's part.

They all looked up as Henry entered, and Lady Quamby straightened and sent him a concerned look.

"Poor Henry, it has not gone as well as we'd hoped, I gather."

Surprised, he halted part way across the Aubusson rug, raising his eyebrows to indicate that she elaborate.

"No suitable bride has presented herself," Lady Quamby clarified. "I'd thought Miss Laidlaw might be a match, but it appears she did not find favour with you?"

"She is a very pleasant young lady, but she does not fire up my senses."

Lord Quamby chuckled. "It is not the duty of a wife to fire up your senses. In fact, far better that she does not. Not when initial attraction rarely lasts."

"I take exception to that remark," said Lord Fenton, looking up. "You forget my own pleasing experiment in that regard."

Henry offered Lady Fenton an exaggerated bow and straightened with a smile. "However, you are wrong that the experiment has not yielded what I'd hoped. On the contrary, I could not be happier."

He saw the faint puzzlement in the creased foreheads of his hostess and her sister.

"You surely can't mean—" Lady Quamby began, but he cut her off.

"Miss Manners is the young lady of whom I speak. Not that you didn't know that." He grinned, unsurprised at their slightly scandalised looks.

"Yes, it's true she is not the young lady of wealth and breeding that the other young ladies are. However, she has attributes that I prize highly. Nor does she have the lofty marital ambitions that I deplore."

"Be careful, Henry. You will soon have a position of importance and a reputation to maintain," cautioned Lord Fenton.

"Love aside, you cannot do anything as rash as offer for someone of whom you know nothing," Lady Fenton interjected. "I beg you, do your own diligence and don't take it for granted that her mere presence here guarantees her credentials."

She flicked a worried glance at her sister, who patted her neatly coiffured golden curls and looked uncharacteristically troubled.

"The fact is, Henry," Lady Fenton went on, "your mother has communicated her delight to me at her understanding that you have lost your heart to a blameless young lady we've harboured under our roof—believing, therefore that she is eminently suitable."

"As any cousin of Miss Manners certainly would be." Henry, feeling cornered, as he stood in the centre of the rug. He heard the defensiveness in his tone and didn't care. He was going to ask Tilly to be his wife tonight and if that meant fielding the objections of the entire company, he'd do that.

Hadn't he himself had to overcome his own reservations? And what had finally broken those down? The realisation that there could not exist any other young woman with whom he could be not only madly, passionately in love, but who would interest, entertain and fascinate him. Tilly Manners had every attribute he prized in the wife for whom he was searching.

The daring, adventurous and unconventional streak that had initially caused his earlier initial rethink was, almost paradoxically, part of the reason for his enthusiasm.

Miss Manners truly was an original. And hadn't he resisted marriage so long because he was so unattracted to the vapid, ordinary young lady who seemed to emerge from the same mould, year after year?

Henry didn't like the long pause, and the clearly troubled response of both Ladies Fenton and Quamby and their respective spouses. All four pairs of eyes regarded him warily, as if waiting for someone else to make a rejoinder.

It certainly wasn't like Lady Quamby to be lost for words.

"Have you met Miss Manners' people?" Lord Quamby asked.

"I'm marrying Miss Manners, not her people," Henry said, perhaps unwisely. This was the first he'd mentioned marriage, and he'd surprised even himself.

But there it was. Having said the word, it was as if he were embedding what had been whirling about his brain from the moment he'd first clasped Miss Manners in his arms.

She'd shocked him on many occasions since then, but, shocked, enthralled, intrigued or whatever else, she was the woman with whom he wanted to spend the rest of his life. He'd never felt that before.

So what did it matter if her 'people' were not as well heeled, well-dressed or respectable as his hosts apparently believed they ought to be if he were to make an alliance with them?

"The fact that Miss Manners is here is enough for me," he repeated, continuing his progress towards an armchair. Relaxing into its comfortable depths, he steepled his fingers and regarded them with a smile.

"The young ladies and gentlemen have acquitted themselves admirably." He cleared his throat. "If, that is, I am to make such judgement in my capacity as their tutor. I'm sure this evening will be a magnificent culmination of their efforts."

Lady Fenton glanced at her sister, and then at Henry. "Did you know your mama will be attending tonight?"

Henry shrugged. "It was discussed as a possibility rather than a probability. No doubt word that my interest had been engaged was a precipitating factor."

"No doubt," Lady Quamby agreed. She shifted uneasily. "So, will you introduce Miss Manners to her, or do you wish me to do so?"

Henry chuckled. "I think you're more afraid of my mama and her reaction than I am, Lady Quamby. By all means, I will allow you to introduce Miss Manners, but leave the rest to me. However my mama reacts, you will be blameless."

He didn't miss the relief in her eye. "Blameless? Then there is no more to be said. Your mama can be formidable and I was merely worried she would consider I had not done my due diligence in inviting to my household a potential contender for you who had not been properly vetted. As you rightly say, Miss Manners is a charming, if unusually direct, young lady."

"Just the way I like her," Henry said with satisfaction, making it clear that he was suffering not the slightest bit of angst in forging ahead with the most important decision of his life, even if it had been made clear that it may not please everyone.

TILLY DIDN'T CARE that she'd worn the pink net gown three out of the seven nights she'd attended dancing after dinner. Henry knew she had limited funds. Henry didn't care, for he was in love and she was more than he could have imagined. He'd told her so, and even with her limited understanding of society's mysterious workings, she knew Henry took a great risk in making advances towards one of Lady Quamby's debutantes.

Just as well Tilly had behaved with such apparent brazenness so early in the piece, or he may never have become emboldened enough to pursue her.

A frisson of excitement ran through her as she worked her long dark hair into something resembling the elegant coiffure Matilda so often sported at evenings like this one. On many a night, Tilly had helped weave pearls through her hair, done up the buttons at the back of her gown or curled and primped Matilda's long dark locks. They were her crowning glory, just as Tilly's glossy tresses were hers. Though dissimilar in looks when studied side by side, there was enough of a resemblance that shopkeepers and others in the village had wondered whether they might be sisters or cousins.

With a few minutes to wait before it was time to descend the stairs and make her appearance in the drawing room, Tilly wondered how Matilda was faring back at home and if she had achieved her heart's desire.

Perhaps in a week, they'd both settle themselves comfortably in Matilda's bed chamber and discuss the events of the past life-changing week, before making plans for each to act as maid of honour for the other.

The gong downstairs sounded, and Tilly prepared to make her elegant descent. She stepped out of her bedchamber and met Miss Laidlaw upon the stairs.

"I like that gown more each time I see it," that young lady said with a disingenuous smile. "Pale pink and dark hair are such an arresting combination." She pretended to walk at her side, her conversation companionable, and although Tilly didn't mind, for she knew she was going to be a great deal happier than Miss Laidlaw when all was said and done, she also the desire to put that young lady in her place.

Miss Laidlaw thought she was so much better than Tilly

and indeed, socially, she was—but Tilly was going to be so much more satisfied with her lot in life.

Soon Henry would ask her to be his wife. She had that feeling in her bones. He'd hinted at it, and he'd overcome the psychological hurdle of discovering she was not the pure miss he had expected. Which was as it should be.

In the drawing room, the young ladies separated, Miss Laidlaw joining her gaggle of bosom friends, leaving Tilly alone in the doorway.

She could see Henry in discussion with Lord Fenton, but of course she could not interrupt. She knew her place in this sphere.

Yasmin and Zena had no regard for a person's social standing, dishing out advice, abortifacients and mystical prognostications to the high quality ladies who appeared, shrouded in veils and secrecy, in their cottage in the dead of night.

Her sisters would deride them afterwards. They'd be full of scorn and mockery for the unfortunate situation many a respectable middle class, or society, lady found herself. Tilly had listened to their conversations—and those they had with their clientele—from her pallet behind a grimy curtain in the lean-to that served as her bedchamber, adjoining the parlour. Lying in these cramped quarters in the dead of night, she'd learned a lot about life and the grim underbelly of these women's lives.

They might go about dressed in silks and furs, but Tilly knew her freedom and knowledge made her far happier than these miserable slaves of convention.

So, while Tilly stood alone for a few moments by the drawing room door, she felt no embarrassment, nor longing to be included in any of the cosy conversations taking place about the room.

She certainly had no particular desire to be taken up by Mr Fortescue, who disengaged himself from his conversation with Lady Fenton and sidled up to her. However, nor did she mind, either. He was dashing enough in his own way, and could make her laugh like neither gauche young Mr Snape or Lord Oxenholme.

She caught Henry's glance, which she acknowledged with a quick smile on the back of a laugh at Mr Montescue's final quip in a funny story. Tilly didn't believe in playing games like making a fellow jealous, though Matilda's words did float through her head as she found herself enjoying the attention of both men.

Pretend to be really engaged, though not quite flirtatious, before swivelling your attention towards the gentleman you really like. But only briefly.

It was as if Matilda had read it in some lady's manual. Again, Tilly wondered how Matilda's husband-hunting was progressing. They'd have lots to share when Tilly returned home.

"Alas, this is the last evening we shall spend together, Miss Manners, if you really do follow through on your terrible threat to eschew London this season." Mr Fortescue was smiling that assessing smile of his, studying her intently down the length of his aristocratic nose.

Tilly shrugged. "As I said, no London revels for me, Mr Fortescue. I'm the country cousin, only here through the kind offices of my better positioned relative. Though that said, I harbour no great desire to deport myself in London's grandest ballrooms and drawing rooms."

"No ambition, Miss Manners? Really, I thought it was the ambition of every young lady to make as fine a marriage as possible."

"To make as *happy* a marriage as possible is my ambition." Tilly smiled. "Very unfashionable, isn't it... to wish to be happy?"

"Miss Manners." It was Lady Fenton, smiling her character-istically charming and welcoming smile as she appeared at Mr

Fortescue's elbow. "I hope you have found your few days with us valuable? And enjoyable?"

"I certainly hope so, too." Mr Fortescue's tone was surprisingly warm, but before Tilly could answer, Lady Fenton turned to the young gentleman and said smoothly, "Would you do me the favour of telling Miss Laidlaw that Mr Garrick will lead her into the dancing this evening?" She hesitated, then added, "Perhaps you would do Miss Manners the honour."

Tilly opened her mouth to voice her disappointment, for she was sure Henry had promised the honour to her. Not that the other young ladies would consider it an honour, she supposed. In fact, they'd all be wildly jealous, as Mr Fortescue was the most eligible bachelor in the room, and almost as handsome as Henry.

Clearly, though, part of Lady Fenton's strategy was to create an excuse to be rid of Mr Fortescue so that she could speak to Tilly alone.

And, to Tilly's surprise, her hostess came straight to the point.

"You appear to have garnered Mr Garrick's especial interest this last week." Her look was speculative. "What would your family think of that, Miss Manners?"

Tilly floundered. What *would* her sisters think of that? She supposed they'd be pleased enough that Tilly had found someone to please herself. They'd wish her well as she embarked upon her new life, travelling the country at Henry's side before he found some occupation that would keep him at home when the children came. On this, however, they could choose the timing. Tilly knew she had the advantage over most young women. Her sisters prescribed herbs and medicinal roots that inhibited conception. They'd always been forthcoming and transparent as to how Tilly could enjoy the pleasures that were out of bounds to the average young debutante or, even, married woman.

"Miss Manners?"

Tilly opened her mouth and forced out an answer. "They would be happy if I were happy."

Lady Fenton nodded thoughtfully. "I do not know your family, Miss Manners, but I am obviously acquainted with Miss Matilda's godmother, which is why Miss Matilda was invited here." She hesitated. "The truth is that I am concerned that they may consider a mere dancing tutor an unsuitable match for you, and will believe I have failed in my duty of care."

"Oh no, do not think that!" Tilly burst out with more force than she'd intended. "Mr Garrick is eminently suitable from my family's perspective. They will not be concerned by his station in life."

"And yet, you are here to learn the arts that will garner you a marriage that will situate yourself nicely and be of consequence to your family. Surely you see that marriage is not only a matter of pleasing oneself, Miss Manners?"

"But..." Tilly didn't know what else to say since she felt it wasn't right to argue with Lady Fenton.

The ticklish conversation came to an end when Lady Quamby glided through the room, murmuring that the musicians were tuning up in the ballroom and would everyone please file through. The other guests were already here and assembled, impatient to see the fruits of Lady Quamby—and Mr Garrick's—labours.

Tilly saw the nervousness flit across the faces of the three young ladies, and heard Miss Laidlaw murmur, "My mama warned she'd pay special attention to my grace and conduct this evening. I don't think I've pleased her in my life, so I can't imagine I'll do so now."

Tilly felt the first stirring of sympathy for the young woman she'd taken against, almost from the start.

At least Tilly didn't have anyone judging her and perhaps

finding her wanting. Mr Garrick was smitten. His every look, words, notes, attested to that.

What a relief it was that neither Henry nor Tilly had an eagle-eyed parent training their critical gaze upon them. Of all the company there that evening, only Tilly and Henry were truly unfettered. It was a reflection that galvanised her courage as she took Mr Fortescue's arm when he presented herself immediately following Lady Quamby's words.

It also was the reason for her burst of excitement when Henry briefly grasped her hand at the end of the first dance during which he'd partnered Miss Laidlaw and whispered, "If I don't magically appear at the end of the evening, then wait for me in the Long Gallery."

Ah yes, the Long Gallery. What an ideal place it was, the advantage of housing such a collection of concealing screens amidst the suits of armour, and unusual artefacts.

It was behind one of these that Henry seized upon Tilly, whom he found waiting with some excitement, kissing her passionately before releasing her, exclaiming, "My darling, darling girl, I didn't think this evening would be so tedious. It was almost as if we were destined to be kept apart by the machinations of our hostesses. I'm glad Mr Fortescue did such a good job in bearing you company."

At his arch tone, Tilly laughed before rising on her feet to kiss him quickly on the lips. "You sound as if you might be a little jealous, but let me assure you, Mr Fortescue holds none of the attractions you do."

Still holding her hands, Henry smiled. "Not even if you consider that Mr Fortescue has so much more to offer you than I do?"

"I'm in love with *you*, Henry, not your pocketbook. I am not in love with Mr Fortescue."

He seemed relieved by this, enfolding Tilly in his arms and tucking her head beneath his chin. "You are adorable. I want to make you the happiest young woman in the entire world. I would do anything to see you looked after, as you deserve, Tilly. You do know that."

"Of course I do, Henry." Tilly smiled lovingly up at him. "I've known it for a long time, even though we've been acquainted only a few days. Besides," she added, "Mr Fortescue's pocket book makes him a daunting prospect – should he show any interest in me, though I am sure that his only in your imagination. His family would see me as a social climber and not worthy on account of my humble origins."

"Does that truly trouble you, Tilly? Your humble origins? Why, you have the connections that would make anyone—even Mr Fortescue—satisfied. You're cousin to Miss Matilda Harcourt. A dowry isn't everything. And it certainly means nothing to me."

"That makes me very relieved, Henry, but I've also thought about how I can be an aide to you in our journey through life. As you know, I'm skilled in using herbs and roots as medicines. I have a gift, you know. I don't mean to boast, but it has been said many a time." Confidently, she went on, "Wherever your tutoring takes you, Henry, I can assist with my gift to add comfort."

He hugged her impulsively once more. "I've not even asked the question, but we both know it's the only thing that hasn't been said."

The air caught in Tilly's lungs and for a moment she felt dizzy as she closed her eyes, refocusing her gaze on his lips, so soft when it came to kissing, but so resolute as he declared, "Nothing would make me happier than if you consented to be my wife, Miss Tilly Manners. Please say you will?"

"Oh yes, Henry!" she breathed, throwing herself into his embrace once more so that, laughing, he was forced to step back to keep his balance. "I want that more than anything!"

"You don't think your sisters will think you could have done better?"

"My sisters don't believe in marriage like I do," Tilly said simply. "Besides, what does their opinion matter? What does anyone's opinion matter other than ours? We're free to make our own decisions, aren't we? It makes us more free than anyone else here, don't you think? We don't have to abide by their scruples. Now, let's celebrate, shall we?" She tugged at his hand, whispering on a giggle, "Tomorrow we leave Quamby House, but let us celebrate our last evening on linen sheets and a comfortable mattress." Tilly put her finger to her lips as she sent him a sly look, which she swivelled towards the corridor where she'd been accommodated.

Freezing, as she heard footsteps.

"Ah, Mr Garrick, there you are!" Disappointed, Tilly stepped out of sight into the shadows as Lady Fenton appeared. "You took yourself off somewhat summarily. My sister has been looking for you. Miss Laidlaw wanted to say something."

"I'm sorry, but I had rather pressing business."

Tilly heard the smile in his voice, and her heart expanded. Miss Laidlaw was no threat, she knew.

"Henry, you haven't really lost your heart to that dark-haired, mysterious maiden who came in her cousin's stead, have you?"

"If you mean Miss Manners, then you are referring to the young lady who has agreed to be my wife!"

Tilly shivered as the thrill of those words washed over her.

They clearly didn't have such a joyous effect on Lady Fenton. Tilly heard a great deal that was unsaid in that pregnant silence. Then, in heavy tones, "Henry, that was most incautious." Lady Fenton's words were clipped. "You have not done as you'd promised your mother and your other relatives who have such a vested interest in the young woman to whom you must ally yourself."

"I will marry her; and my dear mama and whomever else who thinks it's their business will just have to accept that in this matter I will please my heart."

A frisson of concern skittered up Tilly's spine.

Why should it matter whom Henry married? He could, as he had said, do as he pleased. Yet Lady Fenton was taking issue with the choice of wife of the dancing master?

Feeling increasingly uncomfortable as she hid herself, Tilly wondered if she should quietly exit via the shadows towards the servants' stairs without anyone being the wiser. She didn't want to hear more. Perhaps Henry had been a regular employee of Lady Fenton's who thought her handsome servant could do better. Perhaps she had someone else in mind for Henry.

"Please, Henry, I beg you not to be rash. Granted, she is a charming young lady, but she is… well, we don't know what kind of background she has. We know nothing about her!"

"Except that I love her! Was that not the reason for this whole charade? To enable me to find a woman who would love me for myself?"

Charade?

Increasingly alarmed, Tilly felt her ears burning. She should not be eavesdropping, and yet how could she not stay to hear more? Henry spoke of a *charade*?

Did he not really love her? But no, he was insisting he did. Her moment of doubt was galvanised by the knowledge. They'd been drawn to each other from the start. It hadn't been only on her side. Of course not.

"And I have found the woman I want to marry." His voice was rising. He was impassioned but joyful with it. He knew his own mind.

"Henry, you are to become Lord Lomax. You will need a wife who can fit into the kind of life that will be thrust upon her shoulders." Lady Fenton's voice was calm. "Have you told her? Have you forewarned Miss Manners, so she knows the kind of future that lies in store for her? If you want my opinion, and I realised you've not asked for it, Miss Manners seems the kind of young woman who would not enjoy the duties that will be incumbent upon Lady Lomax. She strikes me as a free spirit—"

Lady Lomax? Tilly was finding it hard to keep upright and silent, much less keep her emotions in good enough order to remain where she was.

She felt a sob rising within her, and hastily, but as quietly as she could, managed to stumble through the dark, weaving between screens and ancient artefacts, until she'd reached the doorway that led out to the servants' back staircase.

Only when she was in the underbelly of the house, in a large, unoccupied vestibule, did she gulp in some air and, supporting herself on the dark-papered wall where she hoped to remain undisturbed, begin to digest what she'd just heard.

Henry was Lord Lomax? Henry was not who he'd said he was?

Had she heard correctly? Or had there been something in the lobster bisque and now she was hallucinating?

For a long while she remained in the dark, trying to rationalise the frenzied thoughts running through her mind.

Then, quietly and carefully, she made her way towards the doors that led through the servants' area, hoping to slip into the east wing undiscovered. She needed the sanctuary of her own chamber as soon as she could.

She could hear footsteps, the lights in the sconces along the length of the corridor revealing Ladies Fenton and Quamby in the far distance as they crossed the lobby. But Tilly was shrouded in the dim recesses of an area they'd not frequent.

Unless they were looking for someone.

She swallowed. Well, she had nothing to say to them.

Then, just as Tilly rounded the corner of the corridor, she all but barrelled into Mr Fortescue whose large hands rested on her upper arms to steady her as he asked, "I saw you looking pale and needing air a little earlier, Miss Manners. Is everything all right?"

He had come after her, too?

"Everything is quite all right, Mr Fortescue. Thank you," she said curtly, in the process of disengaging herself so she could evade her hostesses.

But his grip tightened, and he lowered his head. "Are you quite sure? You seem discomposed." His voice dropped a notch. "You know, I'd be very happy to take the air with you, if it would ease your troubles to talk. In view of the fact we will be saying our last farewells." He caged her hand on his forearm while Tilly sent a desperate look towards Ladies Quamby and Fenton, who appeared as shadowy figures in the distance. Surely they had no interest in her? Only in persuading Henry that she was not the right wife for him.

But she was. She was.

What did it matter who Henry was? All that mattered was that they loved each other. Tilly had never felt an emotion so pure and strong.

CHAPTER 10

THEY FINALLY CAUGHT UP WITH HER BUT ONLY WHEN TILLY HAD shaken off Mr Fortescue who, seeing his hostesses advancing with a look of purpose as they addressed Tilly, moved off, making it clear that he'd been in their employ to help run her to ground from the start.

"We were concerned about you, Miss Manners."

Tilly nodded after a brief murmur.

"Are you missing home?"

Again, she nodded.

"Who will come to fetch you?" Lady Fenton sent her an enquiring smile. "Perhaps we will see your cousin Matilda at last. Or her guardian." She cleared her throat. "Or, perhaps, *your* guardian."

"I shall travel home alone, ma'am," Tilly murmured. Though if everything did go according to Tilly and Henry's hearts, perhaps she would indeed be heading towards the border in a post-chaise and four with Henry, she thought with a surge of hope. A sense of unreality as to what she'd heard earlier was beginning to wash over her.

It didn't make sense. She wouldn't believe it.

Until Lady Quamby said, "We'd hoped to meet your people, Miss Manners." She cocked her head. "After all, you have garnered such interest from Mr Garrick."

Tilly met her gaze. "From the dancing master?" she challenged.

There it was. The closest she'd ever been to confronting someone her social superior through her tone of voice. And yet, what did rank matter when Tilly would never be classed as one of them? Not when she had no parents and lived in a hovel with two unmarried sisters and a third who'd had a child out of wedlock.

"Except, as you might have gathered, Miss Manners, Henry is not just a dancing master."

Lady Fenton had seemed reluctant to say it, but now she spoke in an almost tragic fashion as she gazed at Tilly.

Tilly looked at her feet. She didn't want to hear it. It couldn't be true. She didn't *want* it to be true. If she could only turn and run past the odious woman who wanted to lance her with pain, and disappear into the woods.

"Has Henry revealed who he really is?" Lady Quamby persisted.

"I don't know what you mean," Tilly mumbled. She tilted her chin to look Lady Quamby in the eye.

Lady Quamby had always seemed so much like a vacuous, pleasure-loving butterfly, but right now she appeared menacingly intent upon pushing convention to extremes. To Tilly's detriment.

"Has the young man to whom you appear to have lost your heart told you he is to be elevated to a position that will require him to have a wife… beyond reproach?" It was Lady Fenton's crisp words that finally undid Tilly.

Beyond reproach. How thoroughly that excluded her.

"He has told me nothing, ma'am, other than how much he enjoys his work—as a dancing tutor—and that we will do well together." Reaching into her depths for courage, she added, "Henry does not lie." There. Let them come back with a response to that. No, Henry did not lie. He was good and honourable and it would only reflect badly on these ladies for suggesting otherwise.

"I'm sorry, Miss Manners." Lady Quamby's expression softened. She put her hand on Tilly's elbow, but Tilly jerked it away. She would not be cajoled into doing what was contrary to her heart. And Henry's. Clearly these upper crust people did not approve of a union between Henry and Tilly, but what business was it of theirs?

With a sigh, Lady Quamby went on, "This entire event—my *Instruction in the Art of Graceful Accomplishments*"—was predicated on the need to find Henry a bride who would be the helpmate he needs during a time of great adjustment for him. It had not been expected he would inherit the earldom that will be his upon the death of his cousin."

Earldom? It *was* true? She'd not been dreaming it? Henry was to become an earl?

A screaming buzzing sound sounded in Tilly's head. She felt ill but forced herself to listen. What else could she do as Lady Fenton took up the tale, smoothly, while Tilly's head reeled?

With the sun slanting through the windows in the dusty servant's vestibule that led to the courtyard, Lady Fenton looked out of place in her pristine jonquil gown of lutestring as she said, "Henry had no objection to us helping me find a bride. He did in fact endorse the idea of inviting a group of suitable young ladies whom he could observe—but in a role where he was not a gentleman of consequence."

Tilly put her hand to her throat. He'd been part of the charade from the start? He'd lured her into his ploy? Horror made her stumble. Her insides churned, as if a thousand insects were beating wings and thrashing tiny bodies in struggle to escape.

Her mind clawed its way back to the present. Lady Quamby had just interjected. What was she saying? Everything seemed such a blur.

"No, he did not want to appear as a gentleman of consequence when he was so afraid of being husband-hunted!" Her shoulders rose as she threw out her hands in a very gallic gesture of regret. "It is the great fear of a young man of wealth and title, that he is forever the quarry of every eligible debutante and their mama. Henry didn't want that, so he included on the list several young ladies in whom he was interested, including Miss Laidlaw." There was a lengthy pause, then she added, "And, of course, your cousin."

The two ladies looked at each other, pressed their lips together. Then Lady Fenton said with even greater emphasis, for Tilly had so far failed to respond, "Henry had seen your cousin, Miss Harcourt, from a distance, taking the waters last season, and thought her quite charming. As I know Matilda's mama, he wished for Miss Harcourt to be included in the list of young ladies attending our week of dancing and other activities designed to prepare them for the season ahead."

The feeling of horror, desperation... panic did not abate as the story progressed in tones that suggested that, of course, Tilly must be reasonable and understand all this.

But no, Tilly would not, and did not. She didn't know where to turn.

"Mr Garrick is free to make up his own mind," she whispered. Tears had behind her eyelashes but she would not let them see. No, she would present herself as a young lady of determination. If Henry wanted to marry her, then he would do so, she thought with renewed vigour. Nothing these two interfering matrons could say would change that.

Her mind returned to those precious, stolen moments when they were in one another's arms, and speaking from their hearts. Tilly knew there'd been no blurring of the truth when he'd told her he loved her.

When he'd asked her to *marry* him.

The thought galvanised her. Made her defiant as they watched her, waiting for her response.

Finally, Lady Fenton said, "Of course. Henry is of an age where he can make his own decisions. He is a young man of ambition, but he was afraid he'd be hounded by marital aspirants. That's why he engaged us to help him find the ideal wife."

Their eyes bored into her. Tilly didn't want to hear what they said next. But she was pinioned against the wall in a dingy part of the house where no guests trespassed, and where the servants appeared like ghostly wraiths, busily engaged in their tasks, eyes downcast when they saw their mistress engaged upon... what?

Interviewing the suitability of an imposter?

"Yes, Miss Manners," said Lady Fenton. "Henry expected us to invite a selection of young ladies from whom he could select a wife who would be a social asset."

"But he also wanted to be loved for himself, not for his title, his wealth and his position," Lady Quamby added. Her look turned from concern to suspicion as she added, "But you are Miss Matilda's cousin, of course. We are not here to cast aspersions upon your suitability, merely to... prepare you for the very great honour and responsibilities that will be thrust upon your shoulders once you become Lady Lomax. *If* that is what Henry wishes."

The two ladies shared colluding, triumphant looks. As if they'd somehow trapped Tilly.

Meanwhile, the reality was sinking in.

Lady Lomax. Tilly shivered. It was too great a step to take in understanding in too short a time. And yet it was immaterial. Tilly would marry Henry, regardless of who he was.

Because she loved him, and he loved her.

Her confidence and bravado were returning after a brief hiatus. These ladies were making trouble when it was Henry's choice, as they'd rightly pointed out.

Lady Fenton put a hand upon Tilly's sleeve and smiled. "In view of the very great honour Henry is about to bestow upon you, you will need to summon your guardian so that contracts can be drawn up. The occasion of Henry's marriage has been widely anticipated." She paused. Meaningfully. "Your background will, I am afraid, be raked over. It seems it will not matter to Henry that you come with no substantial dowry. My apologies for speaking bluntly, but it is important that we go beyond sentiment for a moment and speak to the practicalities."

"Indeed, my dear," said Lady Quamby, "all that matters is that you do not have any... shall we say... skeletons in the cupboard that may harm Henry as he makes the most of his new position, including taking his seat in the House of Lords."

"Skeletons in the cupboard?" Tilly found herself repeating in a dazed and stupid fashion.

"No need to be so concerned, my dear. An eccentric papa or a crazed uncle, or even some scandal from the annals of time can be glossed over," Lady Fenton said reassuringly. "No, we're talking about anything damaging about *your* past. But as a debutante of your tender years, that is hardly possible, is it now? It's not as if you have some terrible secret or past association that might do damage to darling Henry's prospects, is there?"

TILLY WASN'T sure what she said in response. She barely remembered how she navigated the gloomy rabbit warren of corridors to reach her bedchamber.

In fact, it was only as her head hit the pillow, as if hurled there by a third force, that her mind painfully, then carefully, digested the import of her hostess's words.

No skeletons in the cupboard. No terrible secret or past association that might do damage to darling Henry's prospects.

Until this obliterating conversation, Tilly had never considered that either of the above had applied to her. It was not uncommon for village lasses to find themselves pregnant but unmarried, and none the worse for it after the respective young man stepped up to his responsibilities. The niceties of high society did not apply to girls like Tilly.

Not that she had ever been in the family way. The skills of her sisters in attending to the universal woes accompanying such potential misfortunes had stood Tilly in good stead.

But a past association?

She thought of Ranulf, not for the first time, with a shudder. Though he had charmed and seduced her, it was not this that she regretted. It was the fact she'd been blind to the cunning way in which he'd used her, first to steal from, and then to pave his rise through the ranks of society.

Huddling under the counterpane, still dressed in her evening gown, she pulled a pillow over her head and let the tears fall.

If ever there was a man who sought to crush others to bring advantage to himself, it was Ranulf.

No, it wasn't the fact that Tilly wasn't the pure maiden Henry's family would expect at the very least; it was that with her came the threat of a dangerous, ambitious man, a serpent of revenge who would profit from Henry's love for Tilly in any way he could.

CHAPTER 11

In the yellow drawing room, Lady Fenton and Lady Quamby considered their options. It should have been a day of festive cheer overlaid by a sense of accomplishment, but neither Fanny nor Antoinette relished the task ahead of them.

"How impulsive is Henry?" Antoinette asked her sister. "You know his mother better than I."

Fanny waved a general hand about the room, encompassing their respective husbands who were engrossed in various reading matter and apparently paying no attention to the conversation.

"He wanted a love match, which suggests a romantic turn of mind," said Antoinette. "Now that romantic turn of mind threatens to undo him. Miss Manners is not the delicately nurtured debutante his mama had in mind." She paused. "What do you suppose we should we do?"

Antoinette gave a short laugh. "It's rare for you to seek my opinion on weighty matters, sister. My advice, though, is to wait until we have more information regarding Miss Manners' background. To date, we have only rumours, and so naturally have put the worst possible slant on matters."

"Lady Fenton, a message for you."

The sisters glanced up from their conversation, Fanny's heart ratcheting up a notch to see Fane, the butler advancing, a silver salver bearing a single piece of folded parchment.

"Let's see what our enquiries have turned up, shall we?" she said on a sigh, having thanked the retainer who had now departed. "Read it softly," Antoinette said under her breath. "We don't want our husbands telling us how to proceed when we'll know best."

Fanny nodded, unfolded the note, and began.

Lady Fenton, it was difficult to locate Miss Manners' family home, as no one could tell me of a young lady by that name.

As directed, I made independent enquiries in the first instance, before calling upon Miss Matilda Harcourt, who told me that Miss Manners is the young person from whom she procures her beauty lotions and health-giving potions and whom she now considers her friend.

Miss Harcourt gave this information—and an address—freely, as she did not know under what pretext I was asking.

Upon visiting the cottage in which she dwells, I was greeted by two females, fair of face, but no longer in the first flush of youth, who, upon my describing my symptoms, prescribed various tonics for what they perceived as a tendency to biliousness.

As they attended to my supposed needs, they were forthcoming in their responses to my questions regarding the 'other' young lady who lived with them.

I fear that the news I am about to impart will not be what you wish to hear. The fact is, Miss Manners appears to have no lineage whatsoever. While she is no relation of Miss Harcourt's, nor is she even related to these aforementioned women, nor to anyone else they know.

Apparently, she was given the surname 'Manners', arbitrarily, because of her beautiful manners, having been discovered as a child of about five years old, alone and wandering by the riverbank just beyond the village. Efforts to locate Tilly Manners' parents were futile and, rather than sending her to the workhouse, the girl was absorbed into the family grouping which consisted of, at the time, the two women to whom I spoke—the elder aged three and thirty, her sister a little younger—together with another younger sister, since deceased.

It appears that as Miss Manners had an ability to ape her betters, she was often the 'face' of the sisters' business, and when Miss Matilda prevailed upon her to go in her stead to Lady Quamby's Instruction in the Art of Graceful Accomplishments, *it was the considered opinion of the women to whom I spoke that the opportunity could only be of benefit to her future prospects.*

Fanny looked up, eyebrow raised as she muttered, "And so it would appear. However, there is no question that Henry can ally himself with a foundling. Yes, the child might speak nicely and have good manners, but she could still be the natural born daughter of a—"

"Publican and his doxy."

"Well, I hadn't really thought along those lines, but if she is the natural born daughter of *anyone*, regardless of their place in society—unless he's a prince of the realm for different rules apply to them, as we well know—poor Henry cannot follow his heart."

Antoinette nodded sadly. "Unless there are records of her birth at least, I don't see how Henry can possibly marry the girl, regardless of how much he loves her. Our father was a reprobate and our mother's reputation mired in mud—though that was proved groundless—but we were legitimate, at least, not to mention that both our parents came from the right class."

"The only positive slant is that Miss Manners is not a gypsy, for that would be not only undesirable, but unlawful." Fanny became brisk. "Nevertheless, Henry must be made to realise that he cannot follow his heart in this instance, as Miss Manners well knows. I pity her, for she, too, was under the impression that Henry was, as he purported, a lowly dancing master. She did nothing reprehensible, in my view."

"Except come here under false pretences," Antoinette remarked uncharitably.

"But not to seek a husband." Despite the girl's unsuitability, Fanny liked Tilly Manners. She had gumption and could have passed muster for any one of the young ladies who had been presented for Henry's consideration.

"It's Matilda who has committed the crime," Fanny decided. "I'm quite sure our suspicions are correct in that she sent Tilly in her stead for ulterior motives she wished to hide from her guardian," Fanny went on, adding with a sniff, "Well, I hope Miss Matilda achieved her aim and *is* to marry the young buck who's been toying with her heart."

"Oh, that won't happen," Antoinette exclaimed. "Mr Griggs is a fiendish reprobate." She looked thoughtful a moment before adding, "Fiendish in bed, also. But—" She sighed. "No, Mr Griggs will not be marrying any innocent debutante unless he has a musket pointed at his temple or the young lady has a fortune to equal the Queen of Sheba's. But now, tell me, Fanny, what are we to say to Henry?"

"Nothing."

"Nothing? Why, I thought we were agreed that it's not possible for a marriage between them—"

"No, it will have to be Miss Manners who breaks the disappointing news," Fanny said firmly. "A young man who has lost his heart will not take advice from a couple of meddling matrons."

"We're not meddling matrons!"

"He'll think we are." Fanny grimaced. "No, the rejection will have to come from Miss Manners once she sees how impossible this really is. And when I saw her face fall as we brought up the danger her past associations might bring to young Henry's ambitions, I don't think it will be hard."

CHAPTER 12

Henry searched everywhere for Tilly, following the uncomfortable encounter with Ladies Fenton and Quamby shortly after the dancing had ended. He'd seen her briefly with Mr Fortescue when he'd escaped the interview with his hostesses, who had all but said the girl was unsuitable.

Granted, Tilly confessed she had not the credentials of her cousin, Miss Matilda. But what of it? Every good family had branches that did not fare so well when it came to advancing themselves through marriage or merit. By the same token, Henry knew of many a great family that had benefitted from fresh blood; this positive verdict delivered from a historical perspective. One had to accept that these decisions should not be viewed from the narrow perspective of the here and now.

Then another fear overtook him.

How much had Tilly overheard of his conversation with Lady Fenton? That he was to inherit an earldom when he needed to tell her himself? If so, perhaps her failure to come to him indicated she was fearful of the responsibilities of being his wife? Or considered that he'd been dishonest because of his charade?

He shrugged this off because he had to. Tilly had said she wanted to marry him, regardless of who he was.

Just as he would marry her, regardless of how lowly her family might really be.

Her heart was open and honest and what did it matter that she'd had a taste of the marital bed earlier than she ought? Henry supposed there were other young ladies of supposedly unblemished reputation with similar secrets. Tilly was just more honest.

But even as this reflection came to his rescue, he couldn't rid himself of a vague uneasiness when he thought back to the events of last night.

After his uncomfortable conversation with his hostesses, he'd gone in search of Tilly and found her with Mr Fortescue.

Strange how the sight of that gentleman making overtures had made Henry's normally placid pulse race.

Henry had been in the act of striding towards them when he'd seen Fortescue take Tilly's wrist as if exhorting her to do something. She hadn't shaken him off, as Henry would have expected. But then his Tilly was immensely patient and sweet. She'd not offend any gentleman, and Henry was letting himself into a lifetime of sorrow if he allowed such things to disturb his equilibrium.

He had to remind himself of this as he continued his groggy reflections on last night.

Dragging himself out of bed, Henry washed, dressed, and resumed his search for Tilly.

Returning to the house, he nodded a little stiffly to Lady Fenton when he passed her in the passage, and then experienced a surge of relief and pleasure at hearing Tilly's voice nearby.

Rounding the corner, he was surprised to see her talking again to Mr Fortescue, who loomed over her as she leaned against the wall.

But she broke away with a look of surprise and pleasure when she saw Henry, while Mr Fortescue seemed to dissolve into the background, for when Henry blinked again, he was gone.

"When are you leaving, Tilly? You know we don't have much time," he murmured. She looked so enchanting with her large brown eyes gazing into his and her glossy black hair reflecting the sun. Her silken tresses really were like a raven's wing.

"Oh, Henry, I wasn't sure you meant what you said last night!"

Her brow creased with worry, but then she was in his arms and his lips were seeking hers as their arms twined about one another.

A footfall nearby caused them to break apart and as a servant passed by, they held their breaths before Henry whispered, "Come to my bedchamber, will you?"

"Now?"

"Yes!" he said, and the look she returned made it clear they were both in the grip of something they could not deny. Soon they'd be parted, though Henry was determined it would not be for long.

She nodded. "I'll follow you in a moment."

With as much distance, decorum and decency as their rising passion would allow, they were soon both in Henry's bedchamber, the door locked, before they fell upon each other on the bed.

But kissing was not enough, though she was the instigator of more.

"I can't bear to leave you, my darling," Henry whispered as he pulled off her dress in between unbuttoning his breeches. Intimacy was already established. They might already have been man and wife, but enjoying the best of what lovers experienced in the full throes of passion.

She didn't reply, instead lying on top of him to kiss his

nipples before raising her head in invitation, her gleaming smile indicating she was more than ready for his ministrations.

Her breasts were soft and full. Creamy as he remembered them from their swimming in the river. Was that only a few days before? They'd taken such leaps since then.

"You are delectable," he murmured in between flicking his tongue over first one rosebud nipple, and then the other. Lord, he could drown in her beautiful, soft, luscious body.

A frisson of concern struck him at the memory of Lady Quamby's reservations, and then was gone. He'd go to hell and back to enjoy a lifetime of his darling Tilly.

Now she was pleasuring him, her hand straying to his nether regions, her small hand gently clasping his balls, toying with them before gripping his manhood, his anticipation ratcheting into dangerous territory.

"And you are the most wonderful lover, my darling Henry."

The rising tide of lust and love carried him like a storm-tossed vessel in a raging sea. She was moist and ready for him, but he pleasured her until he heard her gasp and knew the time was right for him to plunge into her.

Rocking in each other's arms, they rode the crest until Henry was ready to explode.

And did, groaning with sated want and need.

"And there'll be a lifetime of this, my love," he rasped as he held her tightly, their discarded clothing scattered about them, the sounds of activity in the corridor making them smile secretly at each other.

"I may not be the right wife for you, Henry. Your parents will tell you that," she said, as she slowly sat up and, with clear reluctance, reached for her chemise.

As her face betrayed nothing that he could discern as regret or remorse, Henry took this to be a prosaic statement that he'd be told he could have made a better choice from the debutantes on offer this last week.

"My parents aren't the ones getting married," he said, rolling onto his stomach to watch her.

Her movements were graceful with no trace of shyness as, naked, she walked to the washstand and poured water into the basin.

Turning to look at him over her shoulder, she said, "They may persuade you to change your mind."

He couldn't believe she was so relaxed with him, cleaning her face and hands with the damp cloth, then bending to continue her ablutions before she shrugged her chemise over her head.

Henry loved the idea that she came with so few precious sensibilities. Any other young woman would be coy and retiring, covering themselves from his view. He hadn't been with a great many women, but there'd been a handful - mostly adventurous matrons—who adopted such pretensions after that most intimate of acts.

Tilly, by contrast, was supremely unselfconscious.

"I don't think there's anything you shy away from, is there?" he asked, grinning at her.

She thought a moment. "I haven't been put to any great tests in my lifetime." A furrow appeared between her brows. "Until now."

Henry rose, dressed quickly, then came up behind her with her discarded gown. He'd be on hand to help her with anything, as their futures stretched wonderfully before them.

"A figure of speech, my darling, since marrying me is hardly a test that you've indicated might put you to any difficulty."

She paused as, now dressed, she was about to make for the door. "These really are lavish apartments for a dancing master," she remarked. "Lady Quamby must like you very much indeed." The smile that seemed to tug at her lips faltered. "Should I know more than you're telling me?"

There was not much time before they must appear before the rest of the company.

Yes, Henry really *should* reveal himself. Would she be overjoyed to be so elevated?

He assumed every young girl's dream was to marry a title and to be dressed in finery. He could offer her so much more than had he been a mere dancing master.

But would she be daunted by the responsibility?

He gazed at her back, his heart hammering with painful anticipation.

"Tilly, there is something I must tell you—"

"You've changed your mind?" Her eyes were bright.

He shook his head. "The truth is that I have misled you as to the reality of my... station in life."

As the sun slanted through the window, picking up the sheen of her hair, and the fine threads of her pale green gown with its embroidered pattern of leaves about the hem. She looked as if she had been born to the role of being his countess.

The furrow between her brows deepened, and she asked, "You're not... a dancing tutor?"

He shook his head, gaining confidence as he said what surely must be the greatest reassurance to her. "I didn't mean to deceive you, Tilly, but the truth is, with my distant cousin at death's door, I anticipate being made the 5th earl of Lomax before too long."

He saw that she was struggling to digest this piece of information. It was both pleasing and disconcerting that she didn't exhibit delight and throw herself into his arms. She wasn't a fortune-hunter; a young miss who'd go to great lengths to elevate herself.

But she wasn't looking quite like he'd hoped she would.

"You will be my countess, my love," he went on, putting his hands on her shoulders. "The same rank as Lady Quamby, in fact. You'll want for nothing. I know it's a great leap of the imagination, but you really *will* want for nothing. Furs, finery, everything you desire will be yours, because it is my greatest desire to facilitate your every wish, I love you so much." He hesitated, not liking the clouds in her eye. "Tilly? Say something."

She shook her head. "I don't know what to say, Henry."

"Are you not at least a little pleased?" He tried to find the right words. "You think I'm not telling the truth? Is that it?"

"I believe you, Henry. Why would you lie about this, after all? But now it is my turn to confess that I haven't been truthful about who *I* am." She lowered her gaze. "I didn't think it mattered since I considered I'd be a suitable match for a dancing master, so there was no harm in it."

"I don't care who you are, my love. Nor do I care about your past and all that you've told me. You're the woman I want to marry."

"But I'm not Matilda's cousin."

He raised his eyebrows then said, "It's of no consequence to me who you are." He really was speaking the truth. "I want you to be my wife, Tilly, and only you."

She pressed her lips together and to his horror, he saw the tears gather at the tips of her lashes. Her fists twined in her folds of her gown. She half turned, as if ashamed to face him, before swinging back and saying almost defiantly, "I come from very humble stock, Henry. I should have told you before. But everything happened so fast—"

"Hush," he said, reaching for her and holding her against his chest. "It doesn't matter." Nevertheless, he felt a faint stirring of concern. Not for himself, but for how he might overcome the objections of his family. But he was of age. He could make up his own mind.

"Henry, I have no father. I have no name. The name Manners was simply made up. I'm an orphan with no record of my birth." She dashed away her tears with the back of her hand. "I should have told you. It was wrong to keep that from you—"

Henry swallowed and, despite the rush of horror, managed, "Not wrong when I was keeping my own secret." The horror was fast turning to gut-wrenching dismay. Tilly had no father? No name? Tilly was a—?

He couldn't complete the thought, his mind turning instead to how he could overcome such obstacles if what she said was true?

Then he thought of the feelings she evoked in his breast with every glance, every caress. That was what was real. He'd sacrifice his birthright before he'd sacrifice that. No, a man in his position had the resources at his disposal to whitewash what was necessary. He'd gloss over whatever might be undesirable about her lineage.

For a second, he drank in her dark, exotic beauty. Her skin was as translucent as a rose petal, her lips the colour of the mulberries he'd plundered and gorged upon as a child. It was how he felt about all of her. She was exquisite and always would be. Barely on the cusp of womanhood now, she would only blossom as the years advanced.

He wanted her now, and he wanted her forever.

Legally. As his wife.

"I don't care about any of it," he said, more forcefully now. "You are the only woman I want to wed, Tilly." He put his hand to his heart. "You make me feel things. Wonderful things. I don't care what you think might be an impediment, as long as you love me. You do, dearest, don't you?"

The tears fell from her eyes as she nodded, though not as robustly as he'd hoped.

"I do love you, Henry," she whispered, "but I fear for our future."

"Don't!" he said fiercely. "What's changed from... a few minutes ago?" He made a sweeping gesture towards the bed with one arm. "Nothing important, for it's the force of our feelings—not my title or your... lack of one that counts," he finished, slightly less forcefully as an image of his parents loomed before him.

But it didn't matter. He would prevail.

She tugged at his sleeve. "The gong went minutes ago, Henry. We must rejoin the company."

Henry looked at her. Her tears were gone, but there was sadness in her expression.

He couldn't bear it however, now was not the time to be sentimental. He must reassure and then he must do what he needed to achieve his life's happiness.

"Yes. I'll put my head out to ensure that the corridor is clear, and you can slip out ahead of me," he said, in a more practical tone. Then, smiling, gentle and reassuring, "Have no fear, Tilly." He squeezed her hand. "I will make sure everything will be all right." Just before he opened the door he asked, suddenly, "You *would* like to be a countess more than the wife of a dancing master?" He tried to dress up the question in jocular fashion and was dismayed when he met no answering levity.

"I don't think it matters what I want, Henry," she whispered as she slipped out into the passage. "Even if all I want is you."

ALTHOUGH TILLY CAUGHT LADY FENTON'S EYE AS SHE NAVIGATED her way through the lobby at the foot of the main staircase, she went straight to her room.

There, she hurled herself onto her bed and cried her eyes out.

It didn't need Lady Fenton to counsel Tilly, in unequivocal terms, that she must give him up.

Tilly would not be Henry's wife, not because she didn't love him.

She loved him too much.

And so she told Yasmin and Zena in a renewed bout of sobbing, when her farewells were but a painful, distant memory. Yes, she'd vowed to Henry, as she pressed her lips to his, that she would see him in London in a fortnight.

She'd told Mr Fortescue the same after he'd unexpectedly cornered her in the rose garden as she was gulping in the fragrant air of the beautiful estate that would hold such bitter-sweet memories.

"I've not seen enough of you, my dear Miss Manners," he'd

said, "though I hope that will be rectified when our paths will no doubt cross once more in London."

"I shall not be going to London, Mr Fortescue."

"You can't mean it," he'd repeated as if the idea were unconscionable.

"I must return home to tend to family business." She smiled. "No London revels for me, I'm afraid."

"And then he kissed my fingertips once again," Tilly recounted to Yasmin and Zena as they devoured her description of every moment of her time away from them.

She'd already recounted the news that the child Becca had given up was thriving and was called Rafe.

Strange, she thought, that they'd chosen not to bring up a blood relation. But Rafe had been an infant, a drain on their resources. Tilly, as a five-year-old foundling girl, had small, clever hands that could bring in extra money.

Now, Yasmin and Zena hoped Tilly could be an asset in a much grander fashion. They wanted her to marry Henry as much as she knew she could not.

"And you felt nothing when Mr Fortescue kissed your fingers?" Zena asked as she shelled peas. "Even though you said he was the most handsome man there? Apart from Mr Garrick, of course."

"I said he was striking. And confident. But I wanted nothing to do with him. Not when Henry was around. Only, at the end, I thought I had to give the appearance of being flattered."

"Why?" Zena asked.

Tilly shrugged. "Because he… expected it. And it would have been rude to have turned my back on him."

"You've not felt the need to behave according to convention before," Yasmin remarked, rubbing the glass orb on the table before her with a rigour at odd with her usual reverence when in the company of so-called believers.

"I think the good manners—or the sort of manners that are

expected—have rubbed off on me. Someone once taught me pretty manners and I suppose they were more ingrained than I realised." Tilly put her head back against the chair in the nook by the fire and closed her eyes. Less than twenty-four hours had elapsed since she'd walked through the doors of the cottage. A changed young woman. The recent five days at Quamby House still felt like a dream.

A strange, convoluted, twisted, ultimately unhappy dream.

"But Henry has asked you to marry him." Zena rucked up her darned woollen skirts to scratch her ankle. "That's what you want. And it's what he wants?" she clarified.

Tilly wiped her eyes. "But it's not possible. I told you before. Henry has a future. His wife will be… scrutinised."

"And they won't consider you suitable because we don't know who you are?" Zena frowned, as if she couldn't believe this was the real reason.

"Well, of course, that goes without saying. But, worse, it won't be long before—"

Yasmin made a noise of disgust. "Yes, Ranulf was a poor choice."

Tilly flung up her head, the memories of the worst mistake of her life churning. "If you recall, there was some prodding from you and Yasmin," she said hotly.

Zena shrugged and exchanged a look with her older sister. "Everyone was looking to take what pleasure they could during those few days of freedom at the hiring fair, and we saw the way he looked at you. He was beautiful! And he thought you were too. Why not lose your innocence to such an Adonis before he was snapped up to make up a nice matching pair of handsome footmen for some sex-starved dowager duchess?"

"That's vulgar," Tilly responded, her sensibilities surprisingly offended by what she'd have agreed not too long ago was as close as made no difference for quibbling. Sighing, she went on, "Well, it was no one's fault. You couldn't have stopped me from hurling myself into his arms if you'd tried. His dangerous fascination was impossible to resist."

"Yes, he did have a strange compelling magnetism and a focus like a wild animal," murmured Yasmin, who herself had not been immune.

"But he took what he wanted, and it wasn't me," Tilly muttered. "He stole from me—"

"Yes, not just your heart," agreed Zena.

"And more than your maidenhead," Yasmin added. "Both of which you gave freely. But he abused your trust and that cannot be forgiven." She grunted. "The man who steals into a lady's chamber to raid her drawer of her life's savings is a man possessed by the devil. And the devil is what he is, though Lady Wylie was not of a mind to call out the magistrate when the same happened to her."

"No, not when her husband *was* the magistrate," Tilly said, tiring of the conversation which had become too painful for her.

Zena put the vegetables she'd diced into a pot and picked up her knitting. "Are you afraid Ranulf will blackmail you once he learns you're to wed Lord Lomax?" she asked. "Does he really have that power?"

"I'm afraid he'll bide his time and wait until after I'm Lady Lomax. *Then* he'll blackmail me." Tilly truly was afraid. "He won't squander the opportunity. He'll humiliate Henry by using me as his instrument. Lady Wylie introduced him to some influential people."

"She should have listened to you before it was too late." Yasmin covered the crystal ball with a purple silk scarf. "But maybe he's wed a rich widow and is content with his lot."

"Ranulf will never be content with his lot," said Tilly. "He will turn that strange, compelling, dangerous magnetism to his advantage. And my Henry will be no match for him."

"You can't refuse the marriage of your dreams because of

your fears of what Ranulf *might* do," said Zena. "Are you certain he is even in the country, much less still alive?"

Tilly considered this with a little spark of hope. "I must find out, must I not?"

Her brief enthusiasm was punctured by Yasmin who said, "He is alive. I heard he had gone to London and become the favourite little toy of a countess."

"Why didn't you tell me?" Tilly cried.

"It was not important." Yasmin shrugged. "Well, not important until now."

Her sisters looked at Tilly with sympathy. "So, what will you do now?"

Tilly closed her eyes. "I will write to Henry tonight."

"To say you can't marry him?" asked Yasmin. "From what you've said, he will do all he can to persuade you otherwise."

"I know," Tilly responded miserably. "That's why I have to choose my words carefully. So he no longer wants to persuade me."

CHAPTER 14

Two weeks should have been long enough to mend a heart broken by an engaging lass he'd known for barely five days.

But it was not.

No, two weeks had passed since Henry had received Tilly's letter outlining exactly why she was giving him up, and still Henry felt a great hollow had been gouged in his chest, now filled with roiling, eviscerating pain.

"I say, Henry! Thought I'd see you around these parts with things livening up. My, you're looking a little liverish. Everything all right, old chap?"

Henry turned at the friendly greeting from his old university friend, Bertie Sumner, and gave a semblance of a smile.

"Not really up to London revels, if the truth be told, but Mama wanted me here as she's launching Emily," Henry replied, continuing past the Inns of Court towards his lodgings.

He hoped he didn't look as glum as he felt. He hoped, also, that Bertie changed the subject.

"Gorgeous gal, that sister of yours. So, Emily's amongst the latest crop, eh? So's my cousin, Matilda. In fact, I'm on my way to pay my respects before she lambasts me for neglecting her.

Being a poor orphan, and all that, she lets no one forget how miserable her life can be." He sighed. "My mama says she's lost her heart to a bounder. Lady Wylie, who's sponsoring her, just sent a message round to ask me to jolly her up. Why don't you come along?" He sent Henry an appealing look. "It'd take the pressure off me. Matilda's a lovely gal, but she's not such fun to be around when she's in the doldrums."

After a lacklustre nod—for Henry had barely been paying attention—he was soon ushered into Lady Wylie's drawing room, whereupon Bertie's cousin fairly threw herself upon him in rapturous delight.

"Darling Bertie, you cannot know how I have suffered these past two weeks!"

With the introductions just effected, Henry was still reeling from the discovery that Miss Matilda Harcourt was none other than the young lady he'd been led to believe was Tilly's cousin. Furthermore, she was the young lady he had seen from afar at Tunbridge Wells and whom he'd asked Lady Quamby to invite.

He could not believe it. For two weeks he'd existed in a world of pain, suffering an unexpected rejection, and not knowing how to mitigate the damage to his heart and wellbeing.

Now, here was his chance.

But Miss Harcourt had not finished her tale of woe. "Mr Griggs played fast and loose with my tender heart, Bertie," she went on, grasping his upper arm as he tried to make his way to a seat, having halted his progress in the middle of the Oriental carpet.

Henry felt awkward in the face of this display of feminine emotion. But his desire to ask questions was paramount.

This young woman, Miss Harcourt, was a close confidante of his Tilly? Could she shed light on why his beloved had told him she could no longer marry him?

He nevertheless had to be diplomatic, for Lady Wylie was

seated in the corner, her expression bland as she worked at some embroidery. She now began to speak, and when she raised her head, Henry saw she was much younger—and more attractive—than he'd first thought.

"Bertie," she said, "do come to Lady Busselton's soiree tomorrow night. As you can see, Matilda is in a state of great agitation, and I fear that if Mr Griggs is present, she may forget her ladylike graces. She tells me she was very naughty and declined Lady Quamby's invitation to be primed in just the kind of behaviour she'll be called upon to display over the next few weeks."

Matilda turned an appealing look upon her chaperone. "You did promise not to tell Mr Collins." She glanced anxiously at Bertie. "My guardian was under the impression that I had accepted Lady Quamby's invitation. Mr Collins is still in Cornwall, you know. Not very interested in anything I do, really, but you know, with no mama or papa, no one is very interested in what I do. Only you, Bertie." She leaned across and squeezed his hand. "You're my most loyal cousin, so you'd not say anything if I asked you not to, would you?"

"Subterfuge is not only unbecoming, it is a sin, Matilda. Your uncle should be apprised of everything you do—or don't do," said Lady Wylie with a sniff, once more absorbed in her embroidery. "He is, after all, tasked with your wellbeing—and your fortune until you are of age. Your fortune is the only reason Mr Griggs showed you the interest he did at the outset." She raised her head, adding in a more cutting tone, "And then some other miss caught his eye with the potential to offer him more."

"It's not true, Lady Wylie!" cried Matilda.

Lady Wylie put up her hand. "Mr Griggs has earned himself quite the reputation. He's a bounder, and I can't imagine why no one warned you."

"My friend Tilly did," Matilda said, deflated as she toyed with the ribbons of her gown.

"Your friend Tilly knows nothing of people like Mr Griggs, so there's one opinion you can discount."

Henry blinked at the fierceness of Lady Wylie's tone as much as the mention of his darling heart's name. He studied the woman as her full mouth quivered and her large blue eyes flamed. Her blonde hair was neatly arranged in a series of artful braids beneath her headdress, a confection of lace. He judged her to be only a few years older than himself and wondered at her role here in London. Bertie had mentioned she was married to Squire Wylie, a long-time friend of his older brother, and that the couple had not been blessed with children.

Henry stiffened. Would he give himself away if he spoke up? Yet it was Tilly who had rejected him, not the other way around. He cleared his throat. "You mentioned Miss Manners was your friend, Miss Harcourt. I am acquainted with the young lady and wonder how she does."

Matilda's eyes widened, and she stared at Henry a long moment before she gave an almost imperceptible shake of her head when he opened his mouth to say more, interjecting quickly, "The weather will be fine tomorrow. Bertie, won't you meet me in Hyde Park and accompany me for a stroll so I can dispel my nerves in preparation for Lady Bonham's soiree tomorrow night?"

Henry was not going to miss an opportunity to quiz the young lady when she wasn't under the auspices of her chaperone, so said quickly, "Hyde Park was just where I was planning to be tomorrow, myself. What do you say, Bertie?"

And when Bertie asked him later, with a narrow-eyed stare, if Henry had so peremptorily transferred his attentions from the young lady he'd purportedly met at Lady Quamby's to Bertie's very own cousin, Henry was quick to deny it.

"My beloved is in fact the Miss Tilly Manners just discussed, bosom friend to your Cousin Matilda," he explained as they strolled back to his lodgings half an hour later. "Tomorrow I plan to quiz Miss Harcourt about her friend as thoroughly as Miss Harcourt clearly does not wish to be quizzed in front of Lady Wylie for whatever reason she might have."

That reason was made clear, as he'd hoped, when, the following day, the three young people sauntered along the gravelled paths, enjoying the sunshine and, in Matilda's case, the interested looks and envious glances of many a person they passed.

For she was indeed a fine-looking girl, neat and well made, with lustrous brown hair swept into a topknot and, on this occasion, wearing a charming gown in pink and white stripes with a leghorn bonnet adorned with ribbons.

She also had a plain manner of speaking, so it was not difficult for Henry to garner the information he sought.

"Yes, Mr Garrick, Bertie tells me you are acquainted with my friend, Miss Manners, but I would not have you mention her name in front of Lady Wylie, who dislikes her excessively."

Miss Manners did not look at Henry when she said this; she was too busy acknowledging all the interested looks cast in her direction.

"And why does Lady Wylie dislike Tilly?" Henry asked, wondering how anyone could dislike his angel, for her lowly origins had no bearing on her sweet nature.

"What? Oh, I don't know. She always has, for no good reason I can discern. Oh! Goodness gracious, isn't that Mr Fortescue?"

Henry felt a jolt of embarrassment but the gentleman who'd turned at being addressed, clearly had been apprised of Henry's real identity for his mouth quirked and, rising from a flourishing bow, he said, "I hope I addressed you with sufficient deference at Quamby House, Mr Garrick. Lady Quamby made me an accomplice from the start when she informed me of the reasons behind her gathering—" he glanced at Matilda, adding

—"which Miss Harcourt sadly could not attend, sending her cousin in her place, I believe." He took Matilda's hand and pressed his lips to her fingertips. "How lovely it is to see you after a good two years, I believe. You did well to recognise me, for I never would have imagined that the schoolgirl I met then could have grown into such a beautiful young lady."

Henry was familiar with the coy blushes his own sister Emily suffered when she was offered such compliments, but was more interested in what Mr Fortescue had to say on the subject of Tilly.

"Miss Manners told me she is not coming to London," Fortescue said, corroborating Matilda's statement. Then, turning to the young lady, added, "Perhaps you can persuade your cousin otherwise, Miss Harcourt."

Henry didn't like the way the fellow's eyes shone with interest. Yes, he would somehow entice Tilly to London and then he'd challenge her with her false assumptions that her lack of lineage was an impossible impediment to being together.

They were about to move on and, in fact, Mr Fortescue had just swept them a deep bow when he raised his eyebrows and said with sudden warmth, "Why, if it isn't my old friend Charlie Griggs."

And then a blonde, handsome gentleman with piercing blue eyes and an aquiline nose was introduced and Miss Harcourt was blushing even more furiously as she found her hand in possession of the new arrival's who bowed low, looked at her intently, and murmured, "My dear Miss Harcourt, I can't tell you how I have missed you since I left your little haven in this fair isle. When I sought you out to say a proper farewell, I was told you had left town."

Henry slanted an interested look at Miss Harcourt, who appeared not to know what to say. Clearly she was a great deal discomposed by the bounder. For it was not difficult to ascertain with only a glance that, despite his best attempts at sartorial elegance, only a bounder would go so over the top in every matter of dress.

However, when he heard Miss Harcourt's heartfelt rejoinder to the fellow who had played her so false, he realised that this gentleman to whom Henry had taken a fierce dislike was, in Miss Harcourt's eyes, beyond reproach.

CHAPTER 15

Since Tilly never received letters—only notes which begged her help regarding herbal potions, or to refine a suddenly florid complexion prior to some society event—she was roused from her lethargy at Yasmin's entrance.

"My poor girl. When are you going to return to your old self?" Her sister looked sympathetic as she sat on the lumpy mattress beside her and handed her the crisp, folded parchment with its wax seal. A piece of hessian plugged a hole in the window and the light was dim. "Is it from your young man?"

A quick glance had dashed Tilly's hopes. She shook her head, while trying not to shiver from the cold, for Yasmin had been concerned that Tilly might be dissatisfied with her old life once she returned to it. "It's from Miss Matilda," she said, opening the letter with a sigh. "No doubt she wants to tell me how marvellous things are in London and how sorry she is that I'm not there, so she could tell me all about it, in person."

But a quick perusal had her squeaking in excitement, "Oh! She wants me to join her!" She glanced up, her eyes shining before she slumped with the realisation of the impossibility.

"Why can't you go?" Yasmin asked, picking up the letter and scanning it. "Miss Matilda asks if you'd consider attending her friend in the role of companion. And that this lady lives in the adjoining townhouse, meaning you'd see each other often." She sent Tilly a speculative look. "Is it because you're afraid that crossing paths with Mr Garrick will be your undoing? Oh, Tilly —" She shook her head. "I don't understand your middle class sense of propriety. Just because society deems you unfit to marry him doesn't mean you can't indulge your passions to your heart's content. You know Zena and I have never believed in marriage. Or, in fact, tying oneself to any man for an extended period."

"Well, I believe in marriage. And if I can't marry Henry, then our love is doomed because I *won't* be his mistress."

"You were quite happy to offer yourself to him on very limited acquaintance," Yasmin pointed out.

"That's when I thought it didn't matter what our respective stations in life were—and besides, how else was I to find out if there was a future for us? You've always counselled that I must discover how generous a man is in bed before I make further commitments."

"True enough," Yasmin said thoughtfully. "It doesn't always follow, though, does it? Ranulf was very generous in bed, but that was a ploy to make you trust him so he could steal from you. Nothing more, nothing less. He was just a grubby opportunist. You mustn't think he's some complicated Lothario bent on revenge. Tell Henry you love him and then let him find a way for you to be together. It really isn't that difficult."

"It is, and I'm not about to get my fingers burned a second time," Tilly said, trying not to cry. "If I go to London, I will see Henry again and it will be *worse*, knowing we can never be together in the way I want because I know how dangerous I could be to his future."

Yasmin made a noise of frustration. "Would you rather stay here, nursing your broken heart with no distractions, than go to London for just a few short weeks where there will be distractions in abundance, as well as your friend, Miss Matilda, right next door?" She squeezed Tilly's shoulder. "You know how generous Miss Matilda is when she wants something. And she clearly has ulterior motives for wishing you to join her." Yasmin picked up the letter again, re-read it quickly, then surmised, "I'd wager that Mr Griggs has put himself back in the picture and she wants you to help facilitate this no-doubt frowned-upon little romance that she knows no one will approve of, given his reputation."

THIS WAS AN ACCURATE READING, a formerly sceptical Tilly found when she stepped off the mail coach and was met with a note from Matilda to say she'd meet her in the gardens opposite the row of townhouses where she was residing.

"You know how much I wanted you to be part of our household, Tilly, but of course Lady Wylie has taken you in such dislike I couldn't even suggest it."

Tilly noticed how agitated Matilda seemed as the two of them walked the perimeter of the gated park. The girl was just bursting with news, but Tilly knew her well enough to bide her time and to not ask questions. No, Tilly had learned how important it was to let her dramatic, excitable friend reveal her secrets in her own good time.

As they stopped beneath a plane tree, Matilda turned suddenly and Tilly was sure she was about to be the recipient of an outpouring of frustrated adoration for her beloved Mr Griggs, whom Tilly had never particularly admired.

Instead, Matilda asked in a burst of frustration, "Why does Lady Wylie dislike you so, Tilly? It would have been so much easier if you could have lived under the same roof as me, instead of next door, tending to Miss Grenville."

Tilly was caught by surprise. "I believe there is a saying along the lines of shooting the messenger," she said with a smile. "Lady Wylie took me in dislike when I sought to pass on some helpful information which I thought would protect her interests. However, she seems to believe that my knowledge of her affairs makes me her enemy, though please don't ask me to go into it, for it was over two years ago." Forestalling Matilda's obvious question, she went on quickly, "As for working under the same roof as you, I would rather be Lady Grenville's companion than your servant, if the truth be told."

This did rile up Matilda, who said archly, "Attending Lady Quamby's house party has given you notions above your station, Tilly." However, as she obviously valued her friendship with Tilly—and certainly the help Tilly might render Matilda during the next few weeks—she was immediately apologetic, adding with a sigh, "But you know how my emotions get the better of me and I cannot keep my thoughts to myself before they're properly formed. You *know* I do not regard you in the slightest way as I do any servant."

"I know," Tilly replied calmly, "and I also know that you are enormously meticulous and inventive in achieving your aims which I gather, right now, are to conduct a clandestine relationship with Mr Griggs—against Lady Wylie's wishes, and, no doubt your guardian's—which you hope I'll help facilitate."

"Exactly, Tilly. You are so clever at subterfuge—as you ably demonstrated at Lady Quamby's," Matilda said, not taking offence. "Why, Mr Fortescue was asking after you in warm terms, and Mr Garrick seemed disappointed you were not in London. It's understandable you would not wish them to meet you under these altered circumstances." She swept her arm about their smart surroundings with its smart new townhouses and manicured park. "It would be embarrassing to be shown up as someone had pretensions to a position that was not yours by rights."

"And whose fault was that?" Tilly asked with some acid, brushing aside a tree branch with some energy as they walked. "I took your place for a few days, wearing your clothes—as you requested."

"Yes, I suppose I did wish it for my sake," Matilda conceded with less attempt at mollification than Tilly felt was warranted. "Still, I daresay you'll want to keep your head down next door so that no one who was at Quamby House sees you. And I'll do my part to save you embarrassment."

"I'm not embarrassed in the slightest. Just because I don't know who my parents were doesn't make me lowlier than any of those I danced with, or amongst." Tilly pushed back her shoulders. "I could be an earl's daughter, for all anyone knows."

"But no one ever *will* know, and so you'll have to be content with being Miss Grenville's companion. Fortunately, she does like you," Matilda said, equably. "And I am very generous with my cast-offs, you will admit."

"Freely," Tilly said with a reluctant smile. Matilda was so very lacking in tact, but Tilly preferred her straight talking to the dissembling and false fronts of many of the young ladies she'd met.

And certainly more than Lady Wylie's outward smiles of gratitude and inner dealings of malice.

She did wonder, however, how she felt about being relegated to the shadows when the glittering world she'd enjoyed so briefly was so close, but so tantalisingly out of reach.

Had it been a mistake to come to London when Henry was here?

She knew she couldn't marry him. *Didn't* she? Therefore, he must not know she was there in person or he would seek her out, and then how would she maintain her resolve not to have anything more to do with him?

Or had she only accepted Matilda's invitation in the secret hope that Henry *would* win her over and they could be happy together?

But could he marry her? she wondered in despair.

"Now, enough of that," Matilda was saying, perhaps seeing her thoughts had drifted away from her friend's own concerns. "I have a note that I would like you to deliver to Mr Griggs. And do wait for an answer. You can do that before you join Miss Grenville for tea. She won't miss you if you're only gone twenty minutes, which is all it'll surely take."

CHAPTER 16

It had been too long since Antoinette had come to London. Acknowledging the smiles of gentlemen she had long since forgotten, she strolled along the broad footpath that ran from Hyde Park Corner to Kensington Gardens.

The sight of so many well-dressed personages was balm to the soul and inspiration for her next meeting with her seamstress.

More than a decade of marriage had only improved her looks, she had been told on many occasions, and there was an abundance of young Lotharios whose attentions bolstered her wellbeing.

She would meet one of them today, that dashing, handsome young man who'd been so unexpectedly elevated to the peerage, and whose story she had recounted to her sister. After a decorous initial meeting at Tunbridge Wells, matters had quickly progressed to a wild intimacy and abandon and Antoinette had happily assured her darling Ranulf she would assist him to make his way in society in any way possible. Well, she already had, she thought, smiling. It had taken long for her to give darling Ranulf the confidence he needed to deport himself amongst those who were now his equals. The poor boy had been tongue-tied when introduced to her.

Ah, but how could she forget the look in his eye when they had literally collided in the Pump Rooms?

The wild attraction had been mutual. What did it matter that he'd grown up in humble circumstances? He was a peer of the realm and his blood was blue, and Antoinette was keen to progress beyond smiles and speaking looks.

She would see that he enjoy the advantages that had hitherto been denied him.

Including her bed.

Twirling her parasol as she admired the glittering Serpentine, while contemplating the nocturnal delights that lay ahead, everything felt truly in balance with her world.

Until she caught a glimpse of a familiar figure that sent her equilibrium completely off course.

"Miss Manners, what brings you to London?" she asked, putting herself in the young lady's path and nearly forgetting her own manners.

Uncomfortably, she reflected on the unhappy morning call Henry's mama had paid Antoinette during which she'd complained that her lovelorn son had threatened to eschew marriage altogether if he could not wed the vastly unsuitable young person Antoinette had introduced to him at her *Graceful Instruction* House Party. As if it were Antoinette's fault that the girl had been there under false pretences.

"Not Mr Garrick, if that's your concern," said the young lady, stopping with apparent reluctance, though meeting Antoinette's look with one of mild defiance.

She was a striking-looking girl, but now that Antoinette had learned of her background and of the magnitude of the deception which threatened Antoinette's reputation as a marriage broker, she felt less charitable towards her than she ever had.

Miss Manners had abused her trust. Granted, she wasn't a

gypsy as some had suggested when her brazen behaviour had been revealed, but she was one of three scandalous sisters who lived immoral lives in a ramshackle cottage and took lovers as they pleased.

Antoinette glanced about to see that no one was watching. Fortunately, Miss Manners was dressed respectably enough. In fact, if Antoinette wasn't in such high dudgeon, she'd have passed comment on the becoming floral confectionary of the girl's bonnet and asked where she'd come by the article. Instead, she said icily, "He cannot marry you, Miss Manners. I'm sorry, but society will not allow it. And nor will the church. I do not wish to break your heart—"

"You could not do that!" the girl said with a burst of scorn that had Antoinette taking her in even greater dislike before the girl collected herself and offered a brittle apology.

Drawing herself up proudly, Miss Manners said, "I am here as companion to Miss Grenville and I have no intention of crossing paths with Henry."

"Mr Garrick is his proper title, though *very soon* he will be Lord Lomax, a peer of the realm who will require a wife of breeding," Antoinette corrected her.

"He is Henry to me, and I care for him too much to bring harm to him through an unsavoury association with me, so have no fear on that score," Miss Manners bit back.

Antoinette didn't believe her for a moment. Miss Manners would not give up on a man who loved her. It was inconceivable she would put Henry's welfare above her own ambition. "He has lost his heart to you, Miss Manners," Antoinette said, tapping her fingers upon the handle of her parasol and hoping Henry's mama did not make an appearance. One never knew who would choose this hour to take the air, to admire and be admired. She went on, "He will pursue you if he knows you are here. But I must warn you that his mama and uncle will do all in their power to ensure Henry does not make an unsuitable match. In fact, they have called me to account for failing in my vigilance when I put forward what I thought were *suitable* candidates."

"I am sorry for that, Lady Quamby—Oh! Henry!"

Antoinette turned at Tilly's surprised tone, blinking with shock as the very subject of their conversation appeared in their midst, a look of even greater shock upon his face.

"Tilly!" he whispered, his expression transformed, as if he beheld a heavenly vision. "You came to London, after all."

Antoinette had to quell the impulse to use her parasol in quite an unladylike manner and positively shoo the undesirable Miss Manners away. Instead, she said the first thing she could think of to avert disaster. "Miss Manners came to London because Mr Fortescue invited her. You do know that the pair have known each other since long before our lovely sojourn at Quamby House. And Henry, I've been talking to your mama this morning who tells me you shall be at Lady Beauclerc's soiree this evening." She turned to Miss Manners, edging her out of the way as she rested her hand upon Henry's arm. "By the way, Miss Manners," she said over her shoulder, propelling Henry forward, and leaving Miss Manners looking uncomfortably abandoned, "Mr Fortescue said if I were to see you I must tell you he would be happy to meet you at Gunther's at 2 o'clock tomorrow."

Antoinette hoped that would put the matter to rest, so was put out when Henry refused to cooperate.

"Forgive me, Lady Quamby but I must speak to Tilly," the young man said rather desperately and turning back; but fortunately the girl knew what was good for her, for bobbing a curtsy Miss Manners said, hurriedly, "It was lovely to see you again, Henry, but I must go."

Then she was hurrying away, dodging the lumbering progress of a cooper's wagon before disappearing into the crowd, leaving Antoinette to face the fulminating look of the young man who had been so good natured while under her roof.

Really, young love could be so tiresome. Antoinette arranged her expression. "Henry, your mama sought me out this morning. Miss Manners has no name, no parentage." She tried to look sympathetic. "Granted, she is a sweet girl, but she can never be the mother of the next Lord Lomax."

He looked conflicted, then a flicker of acceptance seemed to stifle the response Antoinette feared he was about to make.

"I have heard the objection from my mama. Good day, Lady Quamby." He bowed. "No doubt I will see you this evening. Please send my regards to Lady Fenton."

A flicker of regret lodged in Antoinette's belly as she acknowledged she had not been altogether kind. A few years ago, she would have been the first to champion true love, having succeeded in the marriage stakes far beyond anyone's wildest dreams.

But how could she champion Miss Tilly Manners who could never be considered respectable?

Antoinette turned, remembering that her own unfortunate premature pregnancy to Mr George Bramley may have damned her chances of marriage and respectability forever.

And would have, had George Bramley not been Lord Quamby's nephew and heir.

Happily, Lord Quamby had no desire to sire an heir, and so detested his nephew that he'd been delighted to wed Antoinette and cut his nephew out of his inheritance by passing off Bramley's son as his own.

Had it not been for this happy circumstance, Antoinette might have found herself relegated to perpetual ignominy in a damp hovel in Dorset with her mother.

Now, having done her duty and provided Quamby with the heir he needed, Antoinette's reward was that she'd been given carte blanche to conduct her amours as she chose, provided she turn a blind eye to her husband's peccadilloes.

With so many Adonises throwing themselves at her feet—and sometimes at Quamby's, too—Antoinette was very happy with the arrangement; and this latest sojourn in London was as much to do her duty by her husband as to further her latest conquest.

Beneath an elm tree in the distance, she saw young Lord Ranulf waiting for her. Satisfied that Henry had disappeared in the direction opposite to that in which Miss Manners had scuttled away, Antoinette waved languidly, then waited, stroking the feather that swept dashingly from her bonnet, as the tall, handsome gallant strode towards her.

"Ranulf!" she called, her insides roiling at the prospect of the pleasurable afternoon that was in store. "Why, I was sure you'd throw me over in favour of some vapid debutante. London is simply teeming with them at this time of year."

With a predatory grin, her handsome lover squeezed her hand, which she'd rested on his forearm.

"There might be fresh maidens a-plenty to choose from, my love, but only a ripe and luscious damsel with your vast breadth of experience in the art of seduction is guaranteed to make *my* heart beat faster."

CHAPTER 17

Seconds after Tilly had quit Lady Quamby's hateful company, she'd stopped at a bend of the pavement to look back up to where she thought she'd find her former benefactress in conversation with Henry.

The shock that replaced the hopeful anticipation of sharing a last look at her true love nearly made her crumple to the ground.

Ranulf was talking to Lady Quamby?

Not only that, but Lady Quamby was stroking his arm as if he were some adorable creature she was petting.

How could this be?

Leaning against a tree trunk, she watched the pair, despair curdling in her belly.

Ranulf had infiltrated the ton and now his ambition would know no bounds.

Now Tilly could never *marry* Henry. The reality knocked out the vestiges of hope she'd not realised she still harboured until now.

"Are you all right, miss?"

Tilly blinked at the kindly old woman who'd stopped to enquire, then picked up her skirts and ran all the way home.

She was about to take the steps to Mrs Grenville's townhouse when she was waylaid by Matilda, who seized her arm.

"Tilly, you look as if you've seen a ghost." Then, in a wheedling tone, "Or have you come here to tell me you've learned the movements over the next few days of my darling Mr Griggs?"

Tilly pulled away. "I only know that he'll be at the National Museum this afternoon and Lady Beauclerc's soiree tonight." Taking two steps back, she leaned against the railing as she tried to regulate her breathing.

Matilda's brown eyes brightened. "Well done, you're quite the sleuth. Thank you, Tilly. But if your agitation isn't about Mr Griggs, then have you enjoyed a secret assignation with Mr Garrick?"

"That can never happen!" Tilly wailed. "No! I saw a man I knew two years ago—and I won't call him a gentleman, for he is not! But here he is in London, pretending to be one—"

"Pretending to be a gentleman when he's not?" Matilda sounded indignant, then resigned. "Well, men can get away with a lot more than we women—"

"Yes, but he's pretending to be a gentleman to Lady Quamby! How will I tell her the truth?"

Matilda considered this a moment as she traced the wrought-iron railing with her gloved hand. With a sigh, she said, "You should just keep quiet. It's not your problem, is it, Tilly? You often want to do the right thing when really it would be much better if you didn't. Well, better for you, I mean to say, for you shall only get the blame for being what you called yourself before. The messenger. Try not to do the right thing all the time, and I'm sure you'd be much happier." Matilda transferred her gaze to the passing traffic, her attention clearly no longer invested in Tilly's concerns. "Lady Quamby is well versed in society matters and quite able to look after herself." Briskly, she added, "Now, I'm going to tell Lady Wylie that I have promised myself to the widow Grenville next door for half an hour this evening and then I'll slip into your chamber and you can do my hair. No one can get my ringlets looking quite as good as you do, Tilly."

"Lady Wylie will grow suspicious." Tilly spoke woodenly. Her heart was still racing from having seen Ranulf and she was not about to let the matter drop as readily as Matilda would have her do. Matilda didn't know how dangerous the handsome fellow was. Ranulf could get away with it, too. Perhaps he really was related to the nobleman his mother claimed was his father. She'd named his Ranulf, after Lord Ranulf who had travelled with his entourage and apparently spent the night at the Inn. But even if his father *was* the now aged, reclusive nobleman who'd not been seen in the metropolis for twenty years, that didn't mean his unclaimed offspring, Ranulf wasn't a cheat and a liar, pretending to be a blue-blood when he was a bastard.

Just like Tilly was, no doubt.

She stiffened as she thought about the injustice. Ranulf, as a man, had power like Tilly would never have. As a mere female with no name or family, Tilly's future looked bleak, indeed.

Still, she had to do what she felt was right. "I must tell Lady Wylie that Ranulf is in town before she is potentially embarrassed in public," she mumbled, earning a short sharp, "No, you must not!" from Matilda.

"Just leave well alone, Tilly. Now, I want you to make sure you're free between the hour of four and five," Matilda was now directing her. "You can do my hair, then, and, after I see Mr Griggs at the National Museum, I'll need someone to talk to as it's no fun having secrets and no one to share them with. Unlike you, I don't have sisters, or family—"

"To take an interest in anything you do," Tilly supplied, having heard the lament more times than she could remember.

"Exactly," said Matilda. Looking more relaxed, she made a shooing motion for Tilly to continue up the stairs. "Go inside and gather yourself together. Things are not so bad that you'd want to draw attention to yourself. Lady Wylie might be looking through the window for all we know."

Leaving Mrs Grenville's townhouse, Matilda took the steps to the front door of her own lodgings, looking across to add sympathetically, "I'm sorry you can't marry handsome Mr Garrick and become Lady Lomax in a few weeks. He is a handsome gentleman, and I was quite charmed when my cousin Bertie introduced me to him." She extended her hand towards Tilly. "Of course you always knew you could never marry a gentleman but there are plenty of lovely potential husbands who don't require… " She shrugged, adding, "You know what I mean."

And then she was gone, but it was not her last words referring to Tilly's illegitimacy that rang the alarm, but rather her reference to Lady Wylie.

For just as Tilly was about to step inside, she made the mistake of turning to look over her shoulder, just as that lady appeared from around the corner.

"You!" cried Lady Wylie, before Tilly could speak.

The young matron's eyes flashed fire, a molten contrast to her porcelain skin as she advanced menacingly.

"Please, Lady Wylie—" Tilly began. Then, despite Matilda's warnings to the contrary, said in a rush, "You should know that Ranulf is in London and you are sure to see him as he's purporting to be a gentleman of consequence and might even be at Lady Beauclerc's soiree tonight."

Lady Wylie stopped, the fire in her eyes instantly doused. A look of uncertainty crossed her face, before her gaze flickered from Tilly to a gentleman Tilly had not noticed bringing up the rear. It was Sir Wylie, paying the jarvey, unaware that his wife was conversing with the 'village lass' whose herbal ministrations Lady Wylie had once eagerly sought.

"I have no idea what you are referring to, girl," she hissed. "Now get inside and if you cross my path once more, I promise you will regret it. Go!"

Tilly didn't need to be warned twice. Rapping quickly on the front door, she made sure only the back of her head was on view to her respectable neighbours, before she collapsed with relief inside.

CHAPTER 18

Henry wandered about Lady Beauclerc's like a man in a dream.

He was only aware of the intricately decorated plaster ceilings, the massive chandeliers with thousands of beeswax candles because his mother kept drawing his attention to the material, though seemed so disinterested in what was more important: the state of his heart.

"Henry, darling, look at all this! Why, this is your new world!" His mother gripped his wrist, the excitement in her whisper causing something inside him to shrivel, rather than soar, as might have been expected.

Though she'd tried to hide it, Mrs Garrick was as delighted as a schoolroom miss that her son was about to elevate her to a rarefied world she only glimpsed during visits to noble relatives and connections.

Henry's cousin, the current earl, was on his death bed, his condition worsening by the day, though the doctors said it could still be months before he expired. This appeared not trouble either Henry's mother or uncle, neither of whom had met him. And, if the truth be told, it only troubled Henry that he didn't feel more on his cousin's account.

His feelings were entirely bound up in the delightful Miss Manners to the extent he could think of nothing else.

"Yes, mama," he said, woodenly while his thoughts chased themselves about his head.

Of course he couldn't marry her. Henry knew that, but it didn't stop the longing.

"You were acquainted for but five days!" he'd been counselled by all and sundry, and it was true. Two weeks ago he'd not met her and he'd been happy enough, then.

But she'd changed something in him.

She'd ignited a great fascination allied to a great tenderness.

She was like no one he'd ever met before.

But he couldn't have her for his wife and she wasn't going to be his mistress.

"Mr Garrick, I'm told you've already been introduced to Miss Matilda Harcourt," his hostess that evening interrupted, prompting him to immediately ask the young lady to dance.

For, although he knew it was futile to pursue anything with Tilly, Miss Harcourt offered an irresistible conduit between them.

"How does your cousin fare, Miss Harcourt?" he asked, in mildly accusing tones when they were on the dance floor. "She is in London, but not here?"

"I shouldn't have sent her on my behalf," replied Miss Harcourt, without any show of remorse. "But she's close by, and enjoying herself as a companion to an old lady who loves to read. Tilly loves books!"

Henry decided she was as vacuous and pretty in an insubstantial way as Tilly was deep and gloriously beautiful from her artless smile to her inner core.

It seemed against the laws of nature that this young lady was granted the right to be whirled about the room and admired when Tilly, more beautiful and surely more worthy, was not.

Miss Harcourt checked herself. "Goodness, Mr Garrick, I hope I didn't step on your foot! Are you all right?"

Her concern brought him back to earth and he realised he'd winced, but he quickly reassured her with a smile that he'd eaten a bitter almond at supper that was disagreeing with him before changing the subject.

"And there's Lady Quamby, who *would* have been your hostess for the week of Graceful Accomplishments." Henry indicated the vivacious blonde beauty who was accompanying a tall, dark-haired and striking young man with razor sharp side-burns and piercing black eyes.

Miss Harcourt's interest was immediate. "Yes, she's dancing with Lord Ranulf. Have you met him? He's from the north but it's his first time in London since inheriting the title," she replied. "I hear you are similarly circumstanced and this is your first time in London. Do you like it?"

Henry nodded as he observed the degree of intimacy with which Lord Ranulf danced with Lady Quamby. The man was definitely a libertine. He had that look about him. Perhaps it didn't matter, though. For while he'd clearly found fertile ground with Lady Quamby, Henry had also observed during the week he'd spent at Quamby House that Lady Quamby was vastly different from her sister, Lady Fenton.

While Lord and Lady Fenton were quite clearly besotted with one another, Lady Quamby was addicted to amours. Henry was almost certain she'd been carrying on a clandestine flirta-tion with the tallest and most handsome footman at Quamby House.

Now it seemed Lord Ranulf, a man a few years younger than herself, and considerably more handsome than the aged and crippled Lord Quamby, was her conduit for amusement.

"I find London tolerable," he replied knowing he looked too

grim for such an artless remark. Then, despite himself, he asked, "And where exactly does your cousin stay when she's in London? Miss Manners, I mean?"

"She is not my cousin, as you know, but she dressed my hair this evening. She's very deft with her fingers, don't you think?"

Henry tried to quell the memory of how deft Tilly really was before he offered the compliment Miss Harcourt clearly expected. "Your hair is very prettily arranged, indeed. Did you say Miss Manners is staying close by to *you* in London?"

"Next door," said the young lady, obviously caught between Henry's admiration and that of Lord Ranulf who'd just raised one speculative eyebrow at Miss Harcourt.

"She's companion to Miss Grenville," Miss Harcourt added when they'd rejoined one another according to their dance steps. "So you won't see her here, of course, Mr Garrick."

"I know." It was the main reason Henry had no heart for the evening's entertainment, and he felt even heavier-hearted, if that were possible, as he bowed and took his leave.

Crossing the saloon, with an eye to making his excuses, the elegant coiffure of a raven-haired miss caught his eye, gluing him to the spot as she half turned.

"Tilly?" he gasped as she levelled him with a look. The dark-haired beauty put a hand to her raven tresses, her piercing blue eyes framed by two coal arches of disdain as she assessed him a moment before moving on.

Henry did not follow her and there was no point in offering an apology. It clearly wasn't Tilly, however he did petition the first person he knew for information.

"Lady Caroline Huntingdon," supplied Lady Quamby, frowning to see Henry so obviously disconcerted. "I haven't seen her in London since she was widowed two years ago."

"It seems I mistook her for someone else," Henry said, though he wasn't looking at Lady Quamby but at Lady Huntingdon's retreating back.

When he turned, Lady Quamby was eyeing him with distinct speculation. "You clearly like dark-haired beauties, Henry, and this one would make a fine catch. I can arrange an introduction, if you wish. She is in London to find a husband and her credentials are impeccable. The only daughter of Lord and Lady Westaway. She wed Huntingdon three years ago but was married for less than one year before he was killed in a hunting accident." Lady Quamby ran the tip of her tongue over her full pink lips. "Tragic, really, for it was known she loved her husband with an unfashionable intensity for all she appears so very distant."

"Then perhaps she is not yet ready for a husband, as I am not yet ready to wed where my heart does not lead me." Henry knew he sounded stiff. "I am proud enough to want any dark-haired beauty to whom I might be attracted to regard me with a degree of fondness. It was, after all, the reason you held your little charade," he reminded her.

"Of course, Henry." Lady Quamby gave a blithe little laugh. "I'm simply telling you her background. Lady Huntington desires children and for that she needs a husband. She is also extremely well provisioned. It appears you favour dark-haired beauties and this is one of whom your dear mama and uncle would not disapprove."

It pained Henry to acknowledge the truth of her words.

Lady Quamby must have correctly interpreted the look in his eyes for she put her hand on his arm and said, "You must forget her, Henry. Miss Manners stole your heart at Quamby House when she had no right to it, being someone other than whom she claimed." She indicated the retreating back of the dark-haired beauty, adding, "But Lady Caroline would make a fine match. And see how she turned to look at you over her shoulder. I shall definitely arrange an introduction."

CHAPTER 19

It was madness, Tilly knew, but how could she possibly resist when Henry had begged her to meet him in Kensington Gardens near the Cake House?

"Tilly, you came!" His voice rang with joy as Tilly hurried forward to where he waited amidst some concealing bushes, barely able to resist the urge to fling herself into his arms.

"How could I not when you wrote so prettily? Oh Henry, I have missed you so!" She drew back a little, adding firmly, "You must know, though, that I came in friendship only."

His jaw hardened. "Do you really believe the impediments are so great?" He shook his head. "Why, the more you refuse me, the more I'm determined we shall find a way. It's true that when my mama first learned the truth, her dismay was so great that I faltered." He paused, then with added determination, went on, "But only momentarily, Tilly. Today I saw a beautiful young woman who reminded me of you, but when Lady Quamby tried to force upon me an introduction, it only galvanised my determination that you are the *only* woman for me."

Tilly didn't know what to say. They were amid the gardens, hidden from view. Nearby, handsome carriages passed by and well-dressed men and women sauntered along the paths. Henry was within weeks of being on an equal footing with London's finest and yet he *still* wanted Tilly?

Hope made her shiver, and she took Henry's hands impulsively. "Do you really think that, Henry? You're not just being noble because you think you'd otherwise dishonour me because of what some would consider the sins we've committed? Though I don't," she added hurriedly. "Nor do I believe you owe me anything. But—" she sighed. "I do love you so."

"You do, dear heart?" He brought her hands up to his lips and kissed her fingertips. "Oh, but I would like to do so much more," he said with a wry smile before indicating the passing traffic as he dropped her hands. Drawing in a deep breath, he said with studied resolve, "I will come to you tonight. I know where you live. Miss Harcourt told me. Tonight we can be together, enjoying what we did before, and we can make plans. Plans for our future."

His eyes were so full of hope that the last of Tilly's reservations fell away. If he was still so determined, then perhaps there *was* a way for them to be together. Tilly would warn Henry of the threat Ranulf posed, and if he still wanted her for his wife, then perhaps he could think of a way to neutralise Ranulf's evil.

"After tonight's soiree, I shall slip away early and I'll find a way to enter the house if you tell me how and where to find your room," he said. "I know the dangers, but I want to be with you, alone, more than anything. You do want that, don't you, Tilly?"

"Oh yes," she breathed. "And it really shouldn't be so very difficult. There's a sturdy tree branch that almost touches my window. Even I could climb out with great ease if I wished, and although the tree is harder to climb up, its branches are gnarled, I have noticed, offering easy hand and footholds." She touched his cheek. "I shall ensure the casement is open so that you can easily gain access."

Finally, he had to take his leave to make a longstanding appointment. Tilly watched his retreating back and allowed thoughts of a shared future to fill her with hope and happiness.

Henry was not some pompous, entitled nobleman who took what he could get. He was honourable and true.

And he loved Tilly enough to want to take the risks she feared would endanger his future.

But he needed to know all the risk.

Tonight, she would tell him everything.

Only then could he decide what he wanted to do.

But first she would let him love her.

At the very least, she'd have that to remember for the rest of her life.

SHE'D JUST GAINED the gravelled path, her heart near to bursting from both happiness, excitement and trepidation, when, coming towards her, she spied the very man who, in all London, she least desired to see.

No doubt Ranulf did not know where Tilly was. He'd probably all but forgotten her, and he certainly would not have considered her a threat.

Until now.

Tilly cast about her, evading his gaze, which was now focussed upon her. As if she were a delightful toy. Or a mouse, and he was a large, and very superior cat.

She might have successfully scuttled into the crowd, and perhaps he'd have thought no more about her.

Except that Lady Quamby chose just that moment to appear from around the corner. Seeing Tilly, she glided right up to her and put a restraining hand on her arm, saying, "My dear, I know you think me unkind and I concede that I spoke harshly to you when last we met. In fact, since then, I have thought long and hard about your future prospects and although I'm glad you appear to understand that marriage to Mr Garrick is out of the question, I've resolved to introduce you to some gentlemen who would be willing to overlook certain of your deficiencies, once they know you have my backing. For that is what you shall have." She dropped her hand and stepped back, regarding Tilly with a smile. "Yes, there is no need for any more anguish. Your broken heart will be mended in good time. Just leave everything up to me."

And then she was gone, having just been hailed by her sister, Tilly saw; and nor had she caught sight of Ranulf, or Lord Ranulf or whatever bogus name the villain went by these days.

However, Ranulf had made himself scarce, turning his back to supposedly admire the view to the north as Lady Quamby glided by, head bent in conversation with Lady Fenton.

After the ladies had rounded the bend and disappeared, the tall, arresting man strode stealthily into Tilly's orbit, snatched her hand and pulled her roughly off the path and into a secluded part of the gardens where they were shrouded by trees.

"You know Lady Quamby?" he demanded.

Yes, these were his first words to her two years after he'd seduced her with his honeyed words and actions, stolen her virtue, her innocence, and the two gold sovereigns she'd hidden to secure her future.

Tilly would not be browbeaten. "You have been pretending to be someone you are not, Ranulf Cartwright. Yes, I know who you are, so don't try to threaten me!" She was not usually so incautious, but Ranulf was not going to use his height and bulk to intimidate her.

Suddenly, all her fears of the power he had to threaten her future and harm Henry evaporated. Ranulf was a liar and a cheat. An imposter and a man who had broken the law.

And it was Tilly who had the power.

The power of the truth. Even if it meant she damaged her

own reputation and chances into the bargain, Henry had made clear the depth of his loyalty. That was what gave her the courage she needed to step back, slap his hand away, turn on her heel, and disappear into the crowd.

INSPIRED by the two chapters of Mrs Radcliffe's exciting *Mysteries of Udolpho* that Tilly had read to Miss Grenville later that evening, she retired to her bedchamber, heart pounding. At least the dramatic and mysterious events of the novel, and the daring of its heroine, could excuse her obvious agitation.

Setting her candlestick upon the chest of drawers, she examined her reflection critically, unfastening her hair from its topknot and pinching colour into her cheeks. It was a balmy evening, and as she opened the casement window, she breathed in the gritty London air and reached out a hand to caress the tree bough that scratched the window in windy weather.

As the garden at the back of the house sloped upwards, there was not a long drop to the grass below, so she did not fear for the safety of her beloved should he lose his grip.

Fortunately, Henry was fit and agile. He'd manage the tree with ease, she decided, happily, as she pulled her afternoon dress over her head and stepped back into the room, twirling on the thin carpet upon the floorboards wearing only her chemise.

In the distance she heard the clock chime the hour. Midnight already?

It wouldn't be long before he came to her, she hoped.

But what did it matter if she was asleep? What a wonderful way to wake up. In his arms.

AND SO IT proved to be. Tilly was in the deepest sleep when she heard first a scratching upon the windowpane, and then a slight thumping as a body made its way quietly over the windowsill and into the room.

She didn't open her eyes. It was too delicious to imagine Henry sliding into the bed beside her and waking her—or believing he was waking her—with his kisses.

Stretching languidly, Tilly gave a blissful sigh. The mattress dipped as he climbed in beside her and, rolling over, the next second she was in his arms.

"My darling Henry, I never thought you'd come," she whispered, kissing the soft, stubbled skin beneath his ear and snuggling into his embrace.

"And I never thought I'd be able to extricate myself from all the inane chatter I had to pretend amused me," he whispered back, kissing the top of her head as he drew her more closely against him.

"It's enough that you hurried here as fast as you could," Tilly said sleepily. "I was dreadfully afraid you might change your mind."

He chuckled. "I stood beneath the tree in your garden for a long while and contemplate whether you might have changed yours. But when I saw the window open, and the curtains blowing gently in the breeze, I thought I needed no more sign than that. And here I am, my darling." He was silent a moment, then added, "Your future husband."

Supporting herself on one elbow, Tilly looked down at him. "You really mean that, don't you?"

"I've meant it from the start. It's you who've been the difficult one. You can imagine I might wonder if there was someone else."

There was levity in his tone, but Tilly seized her opportunity, and her tone was serious. "There is, Henry, though not in the way you pretend to fear." She saw him look up at her, faint puzzlement in his expression which she could only just make out from the moonlight that filtered through the window. He touched her cheek, waiting for her to go on.

Now was the moment Tilly had to elaborate on what she'd only hinted at before. "You already know there was someone in my past. The man who took my innocence two years ago. I have said little about him and maybe you don't want to hear it, but if we're to have a future, you need to know the worst."

He gripped her wrist. "I don't need the details, Tilly. I know what happens—"

"I don't want to give you the details about that," she said. "I just need to tell you about him and how he gained my trust because… because I think you need to know. Because—"

"Only if you feel you must. I don't need to hear it."

"You do." She sighed. "I already have told you we met at a hiring fair where I was selling herbal potions with my sister. He was very handsome—"

"You needn't have told me that."

She could tell he was uncomfortable, but trying to make light of the matter. Or trying to stop her when he had more important things on his mind, given the limited time they had available.

This was too important an opportunity to let past, however. Only the truth could help Tilly and perhaps Lady Quamby and others, she thought. If they would not listen to her, then perhaps they'd listen to Henry.

She put her hand on his cheek and made him attend to her. "I did, Henry, because he traded on those looks. Not just because he was handsome, but because of his resemblance to some nobleman whom his mother, a publican's daughter, claimed was his father. He had ambition, and I was a nobody, then. But—" She exhaled in a rush. "I'm afraid he'll try to hurt you by using me and publicising our affair. First of all, I'm not the kind of girl anyone of your station should marry on account of being a bastard." She felt him flinch and hurried on. "See, you can't even bear to hear the word, and yet my sisters spoke it with ease, for it was fact, and, to them, unimportant. But of course it is hugely important to you, though you might deny it now. And it's important—and in fact an insurmountable impediment to the whole of society. How *do* you suppose you'll be able to marry me?"

"We'll elope. I'll hire a post-chaise and four and we'll make our escape to the border. Then, with the marriage legally binding, there won't be anything anyone *can* say. You and I will be man and wife, and they will have to accept you."

Tilly couldn't see his expression properly, but she took comfort from the gentle touch of his fingers as he contoured her face. His voice was low and soothing. "We'll have a long wedding tour on the Continent. We can stay away as long as it takes to forget the scandal. How does that sound, my love?"

She tried to sound as excited as he no doubted wished. But she needed to remind him of the practicalities. "The ultimate timing of your unfortunate cousin's demise might be a complication. You'll have obligations that will require you to return to England immediately."

Henry shrugged. "But I'll be Lord Lomax. Neither my dear mama nor anyone else will tell me what to do."

"You do sound awfully grand when you say that. I'm not sure I'll have the courage to speak against you, either, my darling Henry," Tilly teased.

"Is that another way of saying that you will jump to my demands? Shall we practise, because you don't sound like the usual biddable young lady, and I'd like to know that if I snapped my fingers and requested that you remove your chemise and lie shockingly naked beside me, just as you did at the river, then you'd do it?"

Tilly laughed softly. "I'd do it, only because I want to, and on the condition you hear the rest of my tale, later."

"There's more? Do I need to hear it, Tilly?" A faint note of alarm had crept into his tone. Tilly knew he was trying to spare her, but she said firmly, "There is a little bit more and it's only in the interests of a fair accounting that will protect others, that I want you to know it. But, there, Henry—" With a little wriggling, she had removed the linen shift she'd been wearing and now she stretched the length of him and hooked her hands behind the back of his neck and pressed her cheek against his.

"You, I note, have not accorded me the same delights." She ran her hand over the coarse wool of his trousers, for he'd removed only his coat before climbing into bed.

With a chuckle, he rolled on top of her, straddling her as he touched his forehead to hers. "Impatient, are we?"

"I think I've shown exceptional restraint considering the impediments we've had to overcome to reach this delicious point in our story."

"Which has only just begun, my precious." He took her lips and kissed her thoroughly as he ran his hands over her breasts, contouring her waist before reaching lower to pleasure her in readiness.

It was everything Tilly had remembered, with an edge of something deeper, heightening both the warm intimacy and the ecstasy.

"There! We have to get married now, for you have spoiled me for anyone else," Henry joked as he held her in the afterglow. "Now I must be sure I don't endanger everything by falling asleep and being found by the ancient widow in your bed."

"She's not an ancient widow, as you well know, and she'd hardly climb these stairs to find me," Tilly said. "But falling asleep might be dangerous for Maisie the tweeny wakes me each morning with a cup of tea, and there is no lock on the door, so she'd be frightened half to death and likely bring the house down, even if she didn't exactly mean to reveal me for the wanton creature I am."

"Wanton? I wouldn't have it any other way, despite the less than complimentary way *you* use the term. Now, my dear, is it possible you are ready for round two and then after that we will discuss the practicalities of our elopement in the next few days?"

"Elopement? So soon? You really mean it, Henry?" She hadn't disbelieved him, but to hear him talk like this sent shivers right through her.

"I'd like the first thing you think about me is that I'm a man of my word."

He would have said more, but both froze at the faintest of sounds in the corridor, and by the time a muffled scratching at the door could be heard, Henry was out of bed and into the rest of his clothes like lightning. As the doorknob turned, he was over the windowsill and somewhere—Tilly hoped—along that tree branch. The speed with which he'd left was impressive, but the fact that a fall from the tree branch would be unlikely to cause injury was reassuring.

It was only when Henry had made his departure that it occurred to Tilly that she might be in danger. The fact was, someone was attempting to gain entry to Tilly's room.

Would Henry remain within hearing so he could render assistance? Should she scream, now, while she still had the ability?

But when she opened her mouth, her fear was so great that no sound came out.

Until, uttering a noise of disbelief, she heard the familiar, excited tones of Matilda who'd already started whispering her news in a great hurried rush before seating herself on the bed.

"Oh, Tilly, you'll never guess what? Mr Griggs and I are going to elope, only we need your help."

Tilly was rendered speechless. Matilda was in her bedchamber in the middle of the night telling her *this*?

Gathering her wits, she said, "You're eloping? What, *now*?"

Tilly drew herself up in bed, pulling the covers up to her chin. She hoped Matilda didn't notice her discarded chemise, which she'd think very odd, if not scandalous.

"No, in two days's time. Mr Griggs naturally has arrangements to make. We can't get over the border without a conveyance."

She let out a gurgle of laughter, and Tilly wondered if her friend was quite sober.

Instead, she asked, "How did you get in here? And why so late? I just heard the hour called. It's two o'clock. Couldn't you have told me this tomorrow?"

Matilda wrapped her arms about herself in shivery delight. In the faint moonlight that afforded greater visibility since Henry had left the window open and the curtains drawn wide, Tilly could see that Matilda's hair was a little mussed and her clothing somewhat awry. Her gown of palest silk was crumpled.

And there was something else.

"Matilda, where's your gold chain?" Tilly asked, alarmed. "The one given you by your guardian? You were wearing it tonight! He'll want to know!"

"If I've lost it, then it's of no matter, for it was a pitiful gift with a chain that clearly was not very strong." She gave another little giggle. "Anyway, it's less valuable than that other important asset I've lost tonight and which is why Mr Griggs is duty-bound to wed me at the earliest."

"Matilda, have you been… drinking spirits?" Tilly asked, as a waft of brandy issued on the still air upon Matilda's laugh.

"And what if I have? I nearly fainted at tonight's ball, and Mr Griggs gave me something to fortify myself. That's also when I learned from one of the servants of the most marvellous and unlooked-for aid to our elopement." She clapped her hands together. "It was like a sign that our future was entwined and that everything for which I'd dreamed was meant to be."

Tilly sat up straighter in alarm. "Mr Griggs gave you brandy and then seduced you and then together you hatched a plan to elope?" She shook her head fiercely. "No Matilda, you can't throw away your future like this. You weren't in your right mind when Mr Griggs took advantage of you—"

"He did nothing of the sort." Matilda hiccupped. "He said how sad he was that my guardian had taken him in such dislike. At first he'd tried to accept with dignity that we could never be together, but then he realised his heart would never heal from the pain of losing me."

When Matilda began to cry, Tilly said robustly, "Your guardian called Mr Griggs a fortune-hunter, Matilda, and I think I said the same thing. He's interested in your fortune, Matilda."

"Well, I don't have my fortune now and Mr Griggs is happy to have me without it. Think how *much* happier we will be when I come of age and we can live as a respectably married couple without a care in the world and all the money we could wish for. We just have to be patient. Aren't you always telling me I must be patient?"

Tilly sighed. This wasn't the conversation she wanted to have right now. Besides, Matilda's rude entry had shortened her night in Henry's arms. And she'd certainly been patient enough waiting for that.

"Who let you into the house?" she asked suddenly. "How do you suppose Lady Wylie would react if she knew you were sneaking about, alone, in the middle of the night? And to see me? She knows I live here."

"Oh, Lady Wylie thinks I'm tucked up in my bed. *No one* knows I'm here, and that's what is so wonderful about our plan!" Matilda clapped her hands together. "There's a tunnel that leads beneath Lady Wylie's townhouse to this one. I had no idea about it until one of the servants mentioned it in a whisper to her friend while I was recovering from my near faint. I'm sure she didn't think I was paying attention when she told the parlour maid the romantic story of a couple of star-crossed lovers who lived in these adjoining houses and who visited each other by way of a short tunnel accessed from the basement."

"Good lord, Matilda, you have had a busy night," Tilly remarked with an irony lost on her friend.

"I have, rather. For you see, after I'd been conveyed from the ball quite unresponsive, for although I hadn't *quite* fainted, I did enjoy Mr Griggs' attention." She gave a sly grin. "It seems Lady Wylie wanted to leave the ball because Sir Wylie was being somewhat liverish over, I don't know what, and she was only too happy to have a strong gentleman carry me to the carriage. That fell to Mr Griggs, who came along with us and then carried me up the stairs to Lady Wylie's own drawing room."

"Won't Lady Wylie go looking for you?" Tilly wasn't at all sure that Matilda was in a state to know the likely consequences of her actions. It was true that Matilda was silly and thoughtless, nevertheless Tilly was fond of her and she knew that Matilda relied on her.

"Lady Wylie was in quite a state of agitation, so I don't think she'll give me a thought. When Mr Griggs was carrying me through the ballroom, I heard Sir Wylie hiss something rather scandalous to her, and if my husband had behaved like that to *me*, I wouldn't be able to think of anything else."

"What did he say?"

Matilda furrowed her brow. "He said something like, 'You promised me it would never happen again, Louisa. You have dishonoured me once too many times and I won't stand for it'." She sighed, adding, "It was very dramatic and of course they thought I couldn't hear anything because I pretended to be in a dead faint in the arms of darling Mr Griggs who was consulting with the coachman who was opening the door of the carriage. And then Sir Wylie remained at the ball while Mr Griggs and Lady Wylie took me home. Well, Lady Wylie then left me alone with just Mr Griggs and the servants, which is when I heard the servants whispering."

"About the tunnel?"

"First about the fact that Lady Wylie had been crying when she'd left the drawing room. The servants said they'd better see to me without bothering her. That's when they talked about star-crossed lovers, and I overheard the lovely story that will enable me to elope with Mr Griggs in two days' time. For after the parlour maid had fetched Lady Wylie's dresser, and they'd had Mr Griggs carry me to my bed, it seems they both thought Mr Griggs had gone. Only he hadn't, of course. He was still in my bedchamber." She raised her eyes to the ceiling and a blush spread over her cheeks. "Then he showed me how much he really loves me, and afterwards talked about all the dramatic, terrible things he'd suffer in order to have me for his wife." Matilda smiled. "Then we crept downstairs and found the stairs below to the tunnel in the corner of the servants' hall beneath a rug. It's used quite often, for the servants of both townhouses go from one side to the other. And the servants' hall was deserted. I didn't even get dust on my clothes."

She clasped her hands together in sudden excitement. "So, you see, it'll make all the difference, for when I elope with Mr Griggs in the middle of Lady Armitage's ball when no one will notice." She sent Tilly an imploring look. "You will help me, won't you? You know I have always been a good friend, offering you opportunities to advance your future whenever I'm able."

It was true, but Tilly did not like the idea of helping Matilda in this regard one bit. Slowly she said, "Despite everything that happened tonight, I think you should wait a little longer before you decide that Mr Griggs is the husband you want to spend the rest of your life with."

Matilda made a noise of frustration. "I've done all the waiting I'm prepared to do. I will not risk him having his head turned by some other debutante who has more money than me, or who is prettier than me. Not after last time," she added grimly. "I'm going to seize my chance while I have it."

"But that's exactly why you should wait a little," Tilly urged. "Mr Griggs thought he had a chance with Miss Miller until her papa vetoed marriage between them. But do you remember that he only dropped his initial association with you the moment Miss Miller, who has more money, showed him a little interest? It doesn't show him in a very noble light. He certainly hasn't been as faithful as you would want him to be."

"Marriage will change that for then he will be bound to me, and he will have to be," Matilda said firmly. She gripped Tilly's hand tighter. "You really are the most wonderful friend, Tilly, and I shall never forget how you've helped me. All I'm asking is that you let me leave my things in your room in readiness for when Mr Griggs comes to collect me. And then I'll come over here by the tunnel and you can make excuses for me when the coast is clear."

Matilda's use of language made Tilly wonder if her friend was living her own Mrs Radcliffe romance. She certainly wasn't in the land of common sense.

But what could she say? Perhaps the best course was simply to agree while she tried another approach to advocate caution.

Closing her eyes, she nodded weakly.

Meanwhile, Tilly had her own elopement to plan.

CHAPTER 20

Antoinette giggled softly as the feather tickled her breasts; then shrieked as Ranulf took first one nipple into his mouth, then the other, before he rolled her over onto her back. Growling, he bared his strong white teeth and narrowed his eyes.

Antoinette felt like swooning. He looked so wickedly desirable. She wriggled her naked hips, traced his cheek with her forefinger, and murmured, "Enough taunting, my darling! I'm ready for you to plunder me with more than a feather. I'm dying for it, in fact!"

The gleam in his eye was intoxicating. Antoinette loved the way darling Ranulf looked at her. As if he really were a ravening tiger and she a delectable morsel.

"You really want me to gobble you all up?" he asked, in that rough accent of his that sounded even more desirable because he obviously tried so hard to modulate his tones like a gentleman. Well, Antoinette was a patient teacher and there was all the time in the world to teach Ranulf to learn to speak according to his station.

In the meantime, it was just too glorious to feel the sensations evoked by his slavering tongue. She shivered and shuddered and pressed her hand to her mouth to stop from shrieking too loudly.

Although, what did it matter? The servants knew exactly what she and Ranulf were up to.

When finally she'd had her glorious release, and he'd plundered her to his eternal satisfaction, or so he said, they lay side by side, panting gently as they looked at the ceiling.

Antoinette squeezed his hand. "You have been well received, my darling. I think another visit to the tailor is in order. And Quamby's man will kit you out just as you ought to present yourself to the world. A well cut suit goes a long way towards ameliorating a country brogue." With a laugh, she rolled onto her belly and tapped his nose. "I think we'll need another session tomorrow working on modulating your vowels. What do you think?"

"Earl Quamby won't object?"

"Oh, darling Ranulf, you surely aren't worried still about that, are you?" Antoinette loved the crease lines that appeared between his coal black eyebrows. "He'll be too busy indulging himself with his own peccadilloes. No, Quamby knows to leave me alone when he sees that door closed." She pointed to the impressive double doors that led from her bedroom, to her private dressing room, and then into the corridor. "No one can hear a thing, so you really can make all the noise you wish. Growl like a tiger if it takes your fancy. Go on! Terrify me!"

His response took her by surprise, but it was only one more reason he was such delightful company. With a shriek, Antoinette leapt off the bed and ran into her sitting room, pursued by Ranulf who, stark naked, had his arms in the air and had adopted the expression of a savage animal.

When he finally caught her, he whisked her into his arms and strode back to the bed, casting her onto the mattress so he could plunder her all over again.

Antoinette did love lazy afternoons like this.

Finally, after their second bout of love-making, she sighed and said, "I suppose I will have to start preparing myself for this evening. My dresser will attend to me within the hour and my hair will need more than the usual attention." She tickled him playfully. "Especially after what you've subjected it to today. Now, I will see you tonight."

With obvious reluctance, he rose and, sitting on the edge of the bed, looked down at his feet. His expression was suddenly so mournful, Antoinette was caught between delight that he found it so difficult to leave her, and pity that he should feel any pain.

She seated herself at her dressing table and picked up her rabbit's foot paw. Dipping it into the rouge pot, she watched him in the looking glass.

He looked so forlorn. And he had not moved.

Anxiously, she asked, "Ranulf, what is it? Are you not happy after the wonderful time we've had today?"

He seemed to find it difficult to reply. "My angel, you are so far above me in every way. I admire you like the stars admire the moon."

Antoinette couldn't decide whether she liked the poetic way he said these words in his country brogue more, or the lovelorn way he looked at her.

"Yesterday," he said, "I saw you in the Gardens. I hurried to be with you, and marvelled at how you were like a golden goddess, and that so many people smiled and spoke to you. Like moths to a flame." He cleared his throat. "And not just men and women like you. Grand men and women. Of course, you are so kind to those beneath you, too. I saw you address a young woman of inferior status. And the way she looked at you. So grateful and humble that you should lower yourself to pass the time of day with her. In her eyes, you were like a goddess to her."

Antoinette blinked, frowning as she tried to recall who he might mean.

He jogged her memory. "The girl had black hair like a raven's wing and she wore a blue gown."

"Ah, you refer to Miss Manners."

"Miss Manners," he repeated.

Smiling as she turned back to the mirror, Antoinette said, "The girl is pleasant enough, but quite the imposter, I'm afraid. Not that I hold it against her. She attended my week-long Instruction on the art of Graceful Accomplishments in the place of Miss Harcourt, who she said was her cousin and whom I think you met last night."

"Miss Harcourt? Yes, I remember her." Ranulf stood up and loped over to the dressing table. Resting his large hands on her shoulders, he said, "She's a comely wench if one likes them dark."

"You really must not refer to a young lady as a wench," Antoinette corrected him coyly. "But I am very glad you prefer golden haired beauties." She simpered, and he chuckled. "I daresay you should get dressed now, Ranulf," she added, a little worried when she heard the clock chime in the passage.

"Of course." With obvious reluctance, he returned to his clothes, which were strewn about the room, and crouched down. Raising his head, he said slowly, "I had at first wondered if this young lady to whom you spoke was in fact the grander, finer Miss Harcourt. I am not such an arbiter of fashion that I can tell by a lady's dress whether she is the lady or the governess."

"Miss Manners is a village lass. So, perhaps you *could* call her a wench," Antoinette said with a giggle.

"And what is she doing in London if she is a village girl and you exposed her as an imposter?" He looked enquiring as he drew on his trousers, fumbling with the buttons of the flyfall. "Should she not be rotting in a cell?"

"Oh, she didn't commit a crime, although I suppose it is a crime to pretend to be of a superior social class."

"Then you are a very magnanimous woman that you spoke to her so graciously rather than dismissing her with a flea in her ear."

Antoinette smiled even as she tried to hide her frown. Ranulf really was taking his time in getting dressed and Miss Frost would be waiting beyond that door in dreadful impatience, for she was an artiste who liked to take her time in creating wonders with Antoinette's coiffure.

Finally, she said, "Ranulf darling, I hate to hurry you along, but I must get ready. My dresser is waiting to attend to me."

He blinked, then flushed deeply as if only then realising the imposition on a lady's time. "Of course, my beautiful one," he said, pulling his shirt over his head, then putting on his shoes. Quickly he crossed the room, bent over Antoinette, and inhaled the scent of her neck. "Exquisite," he murmured, in apparent rapture, which was satisfying enough to make up for his tardiness.

Halfway to the doorway, he turned. "So Miss Harcourt is the friend of this young village person who she claims is her cousin? Oh, dearest, I nearly forgot?"

"What is that, Ranulf, my love?" Antoinette asked, her foot tapping impatiently for he really needed to be gone if Antoinette was going to create the grand entrance she had planned for Lady Lethbridge's.

"As you know, the bank is taking its time with regard to my inheritance. I don't suppose you'd be so gracious as to advance me as little as ten pounds?"

It was rather a large sum of money for Antoinette to have in pin money, but she made no demur. Ranulf was delightful and so worth every penny. And it was only a matter of time before he'd be in a position to repay her.

"I think I have only five pounds in my reticule, my darling," she said, pushing aside a pair of pearl earrings to reach for the embroidered article that lay amidst a pile of the jewellery she had tried on, then discarded, earlier that day.

"You have seven, but I would not leave you with nothing," he said as she counted out the notes.

"No, no! Take it all. I'll just ask Quamby to be more generous," she said, now ready for Ranulf to go as she could hear Miss Frost making some loud throat-clearing noises on the other side of the door.

Antoinette closed her eyes with a sigh of contentment as he kissed her throat, while one hand closed about the notes and the other insinuated itself beneath her bodice.

"Until tonight, my beloved," he murmured, putting his hand to his heart as he reached the door.

CHAPTER 21

"So exciting, dear." Miss Grenville's little blue eyes shone as she listened to Tilly's reading of the novel that had all but absorbed her for the past three days. "What could be more exciting than to be lost in the forest and—"

She stopped at the sound of the parlourmaid clearing her voice as she crossed the room with a silver salver bearing an envelope.

"Or should I say, what could be more exciting than to be invited to the ball at the last minute?" she amended a moment later as she scanned the contents before looking up at Tilly. "Well, my dear," she went on, "it seems Miss Harcourt next door has made a special request that you attend Lady 's Lethbridge's ball tonight?"

Tilly blinked. "But… Lady Wylie is chaperoning Matilda—"

"And Lady Wylie has agreed, but Miss Harcourt is a very persuasive young lady, I know. Very late notice, but if you can get yourself ready, what young lady lets such an opportunity go by? Even if she has nothing in the first stare. Come along, now. No time to waste."

Tilly was still feeling somewhat dazed when she stepped into the large saloon of the Kensington mansion later that evening.

She'd thought Lady Quamby's ballroom daunting, with its handful of debutantes and awkward, gangly young men. Not that she'd been afraid. Strangers did not trouble her.

However, this was grandeur on a level she'd never experienced. The richly papered wallpaper, the beeswax candles that glittered from the massive chandeliers. If she were the kind of young lady overawed by such sumptuousness, it would have taken her breath away.

Instead, it was the sight of Henry across the room that did that.

Looking as if he'd been born to the life, he appeared as a vision of all Tilly had ever desired in his well-cut coat evening clothes. In profile, his nose seemed particularly patrician. Another word for noble, she reflected. Her own proboscis had been similarly described, and in tones of surprise, given her humble origins.

But Henry was a blueblood and a man who would one day take his place amongst the highest in the land. In the House of Lords, no less.

The thought gave her pause. Did she have the right to jeopardise his future? Should she temper his enthusiasm to align his future with hers? It seemed only right if she *truly* loved him.

Which she did.

But then someone was addressing them, and when Tilly's thoughts returned to the present, it was to see Matilda simpering up at Mr Fortescue whose acquaintance the girl had only recently made since she'd not attended Lady Quamby's week of Graceful Instruction.

And that gentleman was quizzing her with a decidedly interested air, and she was replying with great animation and the kind of self consciousness that Tilly had often noted with amusement only overcame young ladies in the presence gentlemen whom they considered very handsome.

Until Mr Griggs cut in and all but directed her to dance with him.

"I say, rather a rude fellow," Mr Fortescue remarked, sending a baleful look toward the disappearing young buck who, Tilly saw with even greater clarity, was a worthless popinjay, as he escorted Matilda towards the dance floor.

"I fear he is making a very concerted play for my friend and that she has been very much won over," Tilly said, adding with heavy emphasis, "only because Matilda is so unaccustomed to London ways and he is the first man who has attempted to turn her head."

"Then a little competition is what is needed, if not only to teach young Griggs a lesson, for I have met the fellow and I can't say I liked him overmuch."

"You'd better be quick," Tilly said. "Mr Griggs is a man whom, I suspect, has such a great desire to get his hands on Miss Harcourt's inheritance he will stop at nothing. I observed his tactics when he visited his cousin, Lady Wylie, who lives in the district from which both Matilda and I hail."

"A short walk from the chalky cliffs of Dover, as I recall."

Tilly was about to congratulate him on his memory but the words lodged in her throat because there was that man above all others she had no wish to see—Ranulf—bearing down on them, and suddenly Tilly was overcome by the very unaccustomed feeling of wanting to faint from fear.

She'd thought he'd stride by, but he stopped, offering Tilly an ironic bow, then introducing himself to Mr Fortescue.

Lord Ranulf, eh? And if he saw the scorn in her expression, it only fired up the ruthlessness in him, for he was smirking at her, telling her how much he'd missed seeing her at Lady Devonport's last night, and that it would be his honour to lead her into the next dance.

Mr Fortescue seemed to think her acceptance was a *fait accompli* for he immediately excused himself and Tilly was forced to obediently sally forth, on Ranulf's arm, into the throng of well-dressed dancers.

"You certainly know how to play the part," Tilly remarked acidly as he led her with commendable expertise around the dance floor.

He inclined his head as if she'd offered him a compliment. "Your benefactress, Lady Quamby, was as diligent in tutoring me as she was this year's crop of debutantes in such necessary accomplishments for her amusement—or was it Mr Garrick's amusement? Ah, but I have tickled her fancy. A lowly peasant, so recently elevated and in need of tutoring. It was she who came up with the idea." He chuckled. "My, my, aren't *we* a handsome pair, though? We penniless n'er do wells who have, through our wits and good looks, managed to infiltrate—now there's a good word I only recently learned—high society!"

"I have not infiltrated high society, for I have been nothing but honest," Tilly said hotly. "You, on the other hand, are nothing but an imposter, trading on falsities. If you imagine you can sweet talk me into saying nothing to Lady Quamby about the truth of who you really are—"

He stopped her with a quirk of brow and a squeeze of her hand. "No, I give credit where credit is due, and I never thought it would be so easy. However, as we are birds of a feather—"

"We are not birds of a feather! I already told you that."

"Ah, Tilly, love, you don't know how much I've missed yer sense of nobility and that glib tongue o' yours. You are truly original, for I reckon there's no other who wouldn't look to profit in any way they could from the situation."

"Such as when you gained my trust, then took my innocence? Well, I was willing, so I won't hold that part against you. But then you stole from me! Yes, the greatest betrayal I have ever suffered was at your hands, Ranulf, so do not think you can whisper sweet words in my ear and I'll turn a blind eye to all the underhand things you're doing right now."

"I don't reckon that at all, my love. Why else do you think I'm talkin' to yer now?" His smile didn't falter, though he stopped trying to speak like a gentleman. How charming and confident he was. Tilly wanted to slap his face, hard.

"Anyways," he went on, "I thought it was worth me suggestin' you might like to join me in me little lark, considering no one will have you in any honourable way, which is what you've always hankered after but can never have cos in truth yer no better than me."

"Are you asking me to lie and steal?" She felt her cheeks grow warm as her bosom rose in indignation.

"That's about the sum of it. Nothin' to lose, is there? You know what I'm about, and I know all about you. Yes, we are birds of a feather, but together we can go far. Further than we can, alone. And I reckon that, castin' me eye about this room, the truth of the matter is that you really *can't* do better than me. The gentlemen here admire a pretty face, but they won't marry a bastard." He smirked again, and his wolf-like eyes glittered beneath the chandeliers. "I got meself some great contacts, my girl." With a jerk of his head, he indicated Lady Quamby who stood on the edge of the dance floor and who Tilly saw with a jolt, was looking at Ranulf with undisguised desire. A desire so raw that it made Tilly tremble with something undefinable somewhere deep inside her. Did Henry want *her* as much?

She pulled herself together.

"I would never stoop so low, Ranulf," she said on a hiss.

He shrugged. "Thought you'd say as much. Always thought you were too good for the rest of us, didn't you? Well, don't come crying to me asking to change your mind when it's too late."

"Hell will freeze over first, Ranulf," she muttered.

"Shame." He shrugged again. "Lookin' at you right now, I

can't say as there's anything more I'd like to do than tumble you in one of them empty bedchambers upstairs. But then, maybe it's only cos you're so prickly that it's speared my lustful intent. Sad to say, Tilly, you give me no choice. If you're not with me, then you're against me, which means I'm going to have to destroy you."

"I will destroy you first."

"I don't think you will, Tilly. I have friends in high places."

"And so do I. But more importantly, I have right on my side. I know the truth."

"When has the truth ever had anything to do anything? When does the truth count when it's one man's word above another, and friends stick together? It's all about power, Tilly. You ought to know that. And the fact is, that I am a man. Sure, a fraudster, a confidence trickster and all them other names that get thrown around at people like me. But the fact is that it doesn't matter how true that might be, I'm a 'andsome cove, no denying it. And I got a countess who can't get enough of me. So, it matters nought what you are, if you're not a lady of genteel birth in surroundings like this. You're a bastard, Tilly. And a *girl*. Who would believe your word over mine? And, even if they did, would they even *care*?"

CHAPTER 22

Tilly was brought back to the present, not so much by the words as by the concern in their tone.

What a contrast it was to hear Henry sound as if he truly cared about her welfare as opposed to Ranulf, who had spouted such vitriol.

"Oh Henry, I… I don't know what I am, and I don't know if this is the place to tell you what just happened, for I was so excited to be here, but now I just want to go home."

"Someone spoke unkindly to you? Someone from Quamby House recognised you and thought you shouldn't be here? Is that what this is about?" His eyes hardened, and he balled his fists. "No one will ever speak to you with anything but respect when you are my wife. Tell me. Who was it?" He swung around with a look that boded ill for anyone Tilly might point out.

Which was was why she decided to wait, even though she could see Ranulf out of the corner of her eye, speaking to Lady Quamby. There'd be no value in causing a public scene in the middle of the first public occasion to which she'd been invited.

"He's gone now, Henry, and I must stop being so sensitive.

I've always prided myself on being able to look after myself without a lot of fuss and bother."

"Well, soon you'll have me to look after you, and I'm ready to make all the fuss and bother needed if people don't speak to you the way they should." His tone gentled. "Tomorrow, Tilly. Tomorrow night, will you come away with me? I can get everything organised within a day. The sooner we're over the border, the sooner that fuss and bother can die down. Henry gently took one of her gloved hands in his, their backs to the room as they made a show of looking up at one of the paintings upon the wall. "What do you say?" he prompted.

Tilly thought of Ranulf and all the harm he could do to her. All the threats he'd made. He's strike at the first opportunity.

Well, Tilly was as in love with Henry as he was with her, so the sooner she could escape the danger Ranulf posed, the better.

But the sooner Tilly revealed everything about Ranulf to Henry and the threat he posed her true love, the better, for Henry needed to know before he made any plans or decisions.

"It's a beautiful painting, Henry." Tilly craned her neck, squeezing his hand, hidden by the folds of her skirts and his coat. It felt dangerous, intimate, and loving. A precious moment, amidst the bustle of all these people.

Out of the corner of her eye, she saw Matilda coming off the dance floor, smiling at Mr Griggs before Mr Fortescue claimed her for the next set that was forming. Tilly noted that Henry did not ask her to dance. He'd not want to draw attention to themselves. Perhaps he was enjoying this moment as much as she. Perhaps he was weighing up the situation as she was, for they were closely surrounded by small groupings who might have taken a more considered view of their closeness.

"And yes, I will run away with you tomorrow, but only if you still think — tomorrow — that it's what you want to do. I told you there was someone who could harm your future. Well, he is here tonight. I wanted to warn you before, but—"

"Why, Miss Manners, what a surprise to see you here. And Henry, good evening." Lady Quamby greeted them both with a faint smile and Henry unclasped his fingers, as the countess said, "It was good of Lady Lethbridge to extend you an invitation."

"It was, ma'am," Tilly agreed. She was meek, for it would serve no purpose to be anything else.

Lady Quamby nodded. "Miss Manners, please allow me to drag Henry away as his mama has expressly asked that I call him over to see Miss Laidlaw, to whom she is speaking. She is quite charmed by the young lady, as I know Henry was during the week she spent at Quamby House."

Tilly was gracious in her farewells and suffered no pangs of jealousy, only a faint sense of desperation that she'd been abandoned.

But coming to stand before her, was Lady Wylie who, not an hour before, had stonily bustled Tilly into a carriage to convey Tilly to the ball as if it were the greatest imposition that Matilda request she extend her chaperonage to Tilly in view of Lady Lethbridge's charitable invitation to the ball which could only happen if Tilly were suitably accompanied.

The young woman was clicking her tongue, as if it were Tilly's fault she was all alone.

"I didn't think I'd have to keep my eye on you all evening as well," she complained, adjusting her evening gloves and patting a side ringlet into place. Tilly thought the handsome looks were beginning to fade, but perhaps it was just that her expression was sour. As indeed it would be to see that Ranulf was parading these quarters as if he owned them. She wondered if Sir Wylie knew the identity of the handsome imposter. His wife's former lover.

Not that it was a question she could ask, and nor was he a subject she could broach, for Lady Wylie had made it clear she was simply going to pretend nothing had ever happened and that she did not know Ranulf. This was no more apparent than when Ranulf swept by, considered them both with his arrogant, superior gaze, then continued his progress.

With not a flicker of recognition from Lady Wylie.

Oh, but Tilly knew the signs, for blushes were acts of bodily betrayal that Lady Wylie was incapable of hiding.

"I'm sorry to add to your burden," Tilly said. She meant it in more ways than one and did so hope Lady Wylie would soften her stance and treat Tilly as an ally rather than a danger and a threat. She wanted to tell the frightened woman—for she could see that Lady Wylie really was frightened—that her secret was safe with Tilly. She also wanted to say that it had not been Tilly who had revealed to anyone what she knew about Lady Wylie and Ranulf. Two years ago, her words to Lady Wylie had been intended to protect her from suffering the same fate as Tilly had, and not as any veiled threat.

"Well, life is a trial and full of burdens," Lady Wylie muttered, clearly not attending to Tilly, for her eyes darted all about the room. They'd settled briefly on Ranulf who was in conversation with Ladies Quamby and Fenton and their husbands. And once again Tilly felt a jolt to see the orange-bewigged Earl Quamby in his clownish costume, rouged and gap-toothed, bellowing heartily at some joke as he leaned heavily on his sticks. His wife, so young by contrast, looked like an unreachable goddess beside him. And yet, they were clearly fond of one another. Tilly had seen this during the house party, just as she'd seen that they both led separate lives for the most part.

With different lovers.

But the façade they presented to society was one of friendly solidarity.

Tilly could never take a lover. She watched Henry talking to Miss Laidlaw and repressed a shudder. Miss Laidlaw was eminently suitable, but Henry did not love her.

"Matilda! Come here, now!"

Tilly jumped as Lady Wylie snapped at her friend, who was passing by on Mr Grigg's arm.

The young girl blushed, dropped her hand, and scuttled over as Mr Griggs bowed and departed.

"You're spending too much time with Mr Griggs," said her chaperone acidly.

At least on this they were agreed, Tilly thought.

"Yes, Lady Wylie," Matilda said, eyes downcast.

"Granted, he's handsome, but you can do better. Don't encourage him. He's looking for a rich wife. Only heartache will come of it, believe me."

Tilly glanced at the young woman's face. Her lips looked bloodless, pressed together, her eyes flinty as she levelled them on Matilda. "Unions do not succeed if there is too much disparity between the parties."

"But Lady Wylie—" Matilda glanced about the room, which was filled with marriages forged on tremendous disparities.

Tilly thought about the trade that must have been made between Lord Quamby and his countess. And so many others like her: ugly, aged men whose wealth, and a title ameliorated their deficiencies in the eyes of the heiresses who clung to their arms.

Or at least, in the eyes of those marrying them off: their ambitious parents.

Her eyes followed several notables. It was not always the man who was older. The occasional rich widow with her younger, handsome husband was a case in point with regard to the Mullinses, who appeared to be doing their best to avoid one another.

Or at least, devilishly debonair Mr Mullins was steering well clear of his grey-haired consort as he flirted with a group of pretty girls at the edge of the dance floor.

It was all gossip and speculation, of course, and Tilly ought to be above that. But she'd enjoyed an amusing briefing from a few idle minutes in Matilda's company earlier that evening as Matilda had pointed out what she'd heard from Lady Wylie's incautious lips. Really, one would imagine Lady Wylie would have learned her lesson by now, but, clearly, at nearing thirty, she was just as unable to still her tongue when it mattered.

Gliding past them in tragic silhouette was poor Lady Huntingdon, beautiful in an icy, untouchable way which Tilly had mistaken for aloof disdain until Matilda had said that after two years the young woman continued to mourn the young husband she'd lost within a year of marriage.

"I heard Lady Quamby suggesting Lady Huntingdon for your Henry," Matilda had said. "She said that despite mourning her husband, Lady Huntingdon wanted children." She'd levelled a speculative look at Tilly, but Tilly felt no jealousy. However, the topic of children had reminded her that Matilda's lack of caution meant she might have no choice but to wed Mr Griggs.

Did Matilda even know the potential consequences of what she had done?

Tilly made a mental note to tackle the subject of pregnancy when she next broached the subject of Matilda's impending elopement.

Tomorrow?

She caught her breath. Matilda planned to elope the very same night as Tilly.

She tried to gather her thoughts. Why should Tilly think that she had the right to forge ahead with such impulsiveness and ally herself to a man so far above her, when Tilly was trying to dissuade her friend from an alliance upon which Matilda had set her heart?

But then her resolve hardened. Even Henry thought Mr Griggs a fortune-hunter. Matilda had a lifetime of disappointment ahead of her if she wed Mr Griggs and Tilly was determined that was not going to happen.

"Don't talk over me," Lady Wylie was now saying in arctic tones as she clutched the emerald necklace around her neck. Matilda said it had been bought as a reconciliation gift by her husband when the couple had patched up their differences following an indiscretion on the part of Sir Wylie, which, Tilly had also whispered, she'd heard was revenge upon his wife for a similar moral lapse on her part.

Ranulf, of course.

"My apologies, Lady Wylie," Matilda muttered, sending Tilly a desperate, narrow-eyed glance.

"You've both been—"

She would have said more only an elderly couple appeared in their midst, clearly known to Lady Wylie for after various pleasantries, tall, distinguished Mr Marchment patted his wife's arm and announced their departure, but not before telling Lady Wylie how charming she looked.

"I heard your husband say the very same, Lady Wylie," interjected his wife, a sweet-looking woman with grey and white hair. "You look tired, though. Are you sure you don't want to come home with us? We've had a lovely evening, but we're not as young as we used to be."

"No. Thank you," replied Lady Wylie, whose expression had not registered the compliment. In fact, she looked even more fraught. "Perhaps—"

They turned back.

"These young ladies can go home with you if you'd be so kind as to escort them."

"But Lady Wylie, the night is young –" Matilda began.

"And so are you. Far too young, clearly, for grown-up revelries where you do not know how to behave," she snapped.

Even the Marchments looked surprised at her tone, but of course said nothing; merely tried to pretend there was no tension in the air as Mrs Marchment clucked over the girls and said she and her husband would ensure their safety and comfort and that Lady Wylie would naturally enjoy the evening, as she deserved, without the responsibility of two young ladies.

"Well, I never! I hate her!" muttered Matilda as she climbed out of the carriage in front of her townhouse and had a brief moment in which to speak her mind to Tilly before she would be escorted to her own front door.

Tilly shrugged. "I'm sure Lady Wylie has good reasons for being tense and difficult tonight. You mustn't judge her on this evening alone when you, yourself, said how pleasant she had been as a chaperone these past few days."

"Goodnight Tilly," Matilda said, not having time to offer a rejoinder. "I will see you in the morning." She put her head close to her friend's as she added, "Or maybe even before then."

"I'm very tired, Matilda. Don't come over too early," Tilly whispered.

For what if Henry decided to make a nocturnal visit? She'd not had a chance to even say good night to him.

"I'm tired, too," said Matilda, taking Mr Marchment's arm and allowing him to lead her towards the steps. "Sleep well, Tilly," she said over her shoulder, adding softly, "It's probably best we have a peaceful and uneventful night in view of what lies ahead."

CHAPTER 23

Out of the corner of his eye, Henry saw Tilly ushered through the crowd with Miss Harcourt, under the auspices of an elderly couple.

Tilly had craned her head around and was seeking someone in the crowd.

Himself, perhaps?

He fancied so, but then only because he felt so sure of Tilly's regard.

She was true. And she was his.

Well, tonight he would climb that tree branch and make his way into her bedchamber, if only so they could discuss the finer details of their elopement the following night.

Although, if matters went beyond that, what did it signify?

His mind was travelling pleasantly along this course sometime later—for it often drifted back to Tilly, even when he was engaged in conversation with others—when he became conscious of a frisson of unusual activity in the far corner of the room.

There were no raised voices, but rather a discernible disquiet that began beneath the same oil painting they'd earlier admired. It radiated outwards through the throng, where at least a hundred people still gathered.

The indistinct murmur was punctuated by a loud, brief noise of distress, followed a moment later by another, more piercing.

Henry glanced up from the conversation he'd been having with Lord Belcher. They exchanged a look of mild curiosity, eyebrows raised, before returning to the topic.

And then a wail floated across the room, clear and distinct this time. "And my jewelled comb has gone!"

"I say, what's this all about?" Lord Belcher broke off and looked about him.

Henry blinked. The room appeared to be closing in as many in the crowd gravitated towards their corner as the commotion continued.

"Lady Westerby claims her diamond necklace has been stolen," was the information from a gentleman hailing from that direction.

"And Lady Wylie says she's missing an item of value, too," said another. "The footmen are being interviewed in the lobby."

This was surely unprecedented. A series of jewellery thefts in the middle of a society ball? It was clearly mortifying for the host and hostess, the latter of whom was declaring in shrill tones that such a thing could not possibly have happened but that if a thief was indeed in their midst, then justice would not distinguish based on rank.

Henry raised an eyebrow. "Daring," he murmured.

"Courting the noose," Lord Belcher said with more energy, when he discovered his time piece was missing. Henry checked that nothing of his had been taken. But then, he didn't have much of great value.

Tomorrow that would change. His material worth might not for a few weeks to come, but his spiritual wellbeing would be enhanced by having at his side the wife of his dreams.

He thought about leaving the ball now and making his way

directly to Tilly's. But then he remembered Matilda had been at her side and he wondered if the two young ladies would be up half the night discussing their excitement over this evening.

Perhaps he'd leave Tilly to her rest for this last night. After all, there'd not be much sleep once they were on the road and heading north. And then for the days and weeks of their honeymoon tour, when they could satiate themselves in each other's arms.

TILLY DIDN'T KNOW how she would sleep that night. The excitement of eloping tomorrow was fierce and keen; but she had no doubt about the rightness of their decision.

If Tilly was judged for failing to have the proper lineage to do Henry justice, she was determined to make up for it in every other way.

Of course, she did sleep. Almost instantly.

But woke to a loud rapping on her door before it was unceremoniously thrust open.

Expecting to see one of the servants acting as emissary for an urgent request that she read the next chapter of The Mysteries of Udolpho, Tilly was surprised to see Miss Grenville herself.

But perhaps this was one of those moments when Miss Grenville was a slave to her desperate impulse to learn what happened next in the stories which consumed her.

Tilly struggled up onto her pillows.

Miss Granville didn't look desperate. She looked frightened and uncertain.

And she was flanked by the unexpected personages Lady Quamby and Lady Wylie. Behind these three figures was, to Tilly's horror, an elderly gentleman with a florid complexion and a bulbous nose. He had a large, grubby handkerchief with which he was wiping rheumy eyes but he took his opportunity to gawp at Tilly when the two Ladies broke ranks, Lady Wylie marching forward and saying menacingly, "You're more of a fool than I thought not to have slipped away into the night by now and made your escape. Did you truly not think someone would come to your room this very morning and discover your crime?"

Tilly was now very much awake. She sat up straighter, forgetting about the covers which left her neckline bare; respectable enough, although the fact that her linen nightgown was on display was clearly an inciting factor in the consideration of the gentleman who blinked rapidly and said in a wheezy voice, "So many vices in such a young person. A thief and a seductress. I will have her dealt with accordingly."

His words elicited a frown of concern from Lady Quamby—though not Lady Wylie.

But it was Miss Grenville who said querulously, "Neither is proved, surely, Sir Bradbury. Miss Manners has always been such a good girl. I did think we should have allowed her to state her case first."

But Sir Bradbury—whose identity was only now revealed to Tilly as the local magistrate—dismissed the old lady's words before levelling a beetling look at Tilly to say, "We will now search the room, Miss Manners. Please get out of bed."

Severely discomposed, Tilly now thought it wise to play the modesty card.

"I will not get out of bed in just my nightclothes with a gentleman present," she said with dignity.

And when it was agreed that Sir Bradbury would quit the room while Tilly put on her dressing gown, she managed to banish all of them except Miss Grenville, whom she petitioned for information in a voice that barely hid her panic.

"Whatever I am supposed to have done, I am not guilty of

theft. I would never steal, Miss Grenville. Not from you, not from anyone!"

Miss Grenville looked deeply upset as she patted Tilly's arm. "I'm sure you would not, my dear, though the truth is, I didn't know what to think when those three personages appeared at my door just now."

"But what do they accuse me of stealing? I cannot imagine what they think they will find in my bedchamber when I've done nothing since last night's ball except sleep."

"Last night's ball. Exactly," said Miss Grenville. "Lady Wylie made some accusations I cannot countenance, but which I'm sure will prove groundless when Sir Bradbury conducts his investigation."

"Lady Wylie did?" Tilly stiffened and clutched the bedhead as she looked wildly about her. No, Lady Wylie could not have anything with which to level at Tilly. Still—

A loud rap sounded upon the door. "Miss Grenville, Miss Manners, I'm afraid I cannot allow you longer. I must gain admittance now."

"No need to fear, my child, if you are innocent," Miss Grenville soothed. "I'm sure it's all a terrible misunderstanding and that by tonight you'll have forgotten there was any unpleasantness as you read the next instalment of the *Mysteries of Udolpho*. That's the only unpleasantness we want in life. Between the pages of a book."

Her reassurances were well meant, but Tilly had no time for any rejoinder. Or to make the assertion that if Lady Wylie had anything to do with this investigation, then Tilly could only think the case against her was deeply flawed.

Then the door was unceremoniously thrust open, and the other three people pushed themselves into the room.

"Please! I can't imagine why you're all here and what your complaint is!" Tilly cried as Sir Bradbury pulled back her pillow as if she'd been secreting a diamond necklace beneath it.

Sir Bradbury turned. "Last night several items were stolen from some of those attending Lady Lethbridge's ball."

"But I left early," Tilly protested. "With Miss Harcourt."

"Yes, you left early. And you were *seen*," Lady Wylie said ominously.

"What do you mean I was seen? Doing what? By whom?"

"I saw you." Lady Wylie straightened, and her eyes shifted from Tilly's frightened gaze to Lady Quamby. "Your companion corroborated the fact you were heard to admire Lady Huntingdon's jewelled clip before it disappeared shortly afterwards."

"Who says they heard this? I don't even know who Lady Huntingdon is. I never said such a thing! Nor did I take anything."

"It doesn't matter who said this or corroborated that. All that's important is that we search your chamber."

Realisation struck, and Tilly gasped. "It was Ranulf, wasn't it?"

"*Ranulf?* You mean *Lord* Ranulf," said Lady Quamby. "Such familiarity! He said you were a loose piece. Not that I'm not partly to blame for allowing you under my roof without doing my due diligence."

"He's not *Lord* Ranulf!" Tilly cried. "Maybe his father was, but his mother was the publican's daughter at the *Ship's Anvil* in Elham. He trades on his resemblance to Lord Ranulf who has not been seen in London for half a century."

"Don't be ridiculous!" Lady Wylie swung round, her face fiery red, as if she feared she were about to be exposed next; something Tilly might have done had Sir Bradbury not uttered a triumphant cry as he pulled from under the bed a reticule filled with, as it turned out, trinkets that were obviously of no greatly valuable, yet were likely beyond Tilly's ability to afford."

"That's not mine." Tilly shook her head and wondered what she ought to say with regard to the belongings Matilda had obviously hidden.

"No, they are not! So, you admit to the theft?"

Panic was beginning to get the better of her. "I was looking after it for a friend."

Lady Wylie let out a burst of laughter, just as she retrieved an emerald necklace from a silk lined bag that was hidden in the pages of a book. "Just like you were looking after *my* necklace for a friend?" she asked. "And this?" she added, as she snatched up a masculine gold time piece. "Come now, Miss Manners? How credulous do you suppose us? You realise the penalties for theft. Please don't add lying to the list of your crimes."

Tilly turned to petition Miss Grenville but the old lady looked as shocked as Lady Quamby.

"I didn't take any of this," Tilly whispered. "Someone must have put it in my bedchamber in order to blame me for it. And I know who did, if you'll allow me the opportunity to prove it."

But her accusers dismissed this.

Sir Bradbury raised himself creakily and gripped Tilly's wrist with fat fingers as he turned towards the door. "You're coming with me, Miss Manners."

"No, I can't. I need to tell someone what has happened. Surely I'm allowed to petition someone for help?"

"Not now, Miss Manners. My carriage is waiting. I will interview you at my address in Mayfair before charges are laid."

He dropped her arm, turning on his heel to go to the window to push down the casement with a bang. "Miss Grenville, stay with Miss Manners until she is dressed. I expect to see you both downstairs within ten minutes. No escaping, my dear. Though I'm sure you know that escape would harden the case against you and almost guarantee you'd swing."

Miss Grenville uttered a little cry of alarm. Even Lady Quamby blanched.

Tilly gripped the edge of the washstand for support. "Please, Miss Grenville, can you take a message to someone to let them know what has happened," she begged. "I'm not asking for help to escape, only to notify someone who needs to know what terrible trouble I'm in."

And even though the old lady looked reluctant at first, there was a flicker in her eyes when Tilly added, "If you could only do that, you would be as resourceful as Ludovico in *Mysteries of Udolpho* and I would forever be in your debt. For the truth is that I am innocent, but I know who has done this to me. And when my name is cleared and everyone is begging my pardon, the real perpetrator will be languishing behind bars." She swallowed. "All that stands between my possibly hanging or being deported and justice is you taking this note to its recipient."

Hastily scratching a message to Henry, Tilly pressed it into Miss Grenville's palm, not quite finished as she heard footsteps marching down the corridor.

Then, obediently, she began to dress.

CHAPTER 24

Or rather, tonight was the night.

Despite having had just a few hours' sleep following Lady Lethridge's ball, Henry gave up trying for more rest when he knew how much he had to do.

Putting on his banyan, he descended the stairs, the noise from the street drawing him through his drawing room to the open casement.

Despite the early hour, the thoroughfare below was teeming with activity, a noisy group of vagabonds toasting acorns just below his window. Coughing as he breathed in a gust of sooty air, Henry closed the casement and thought of that other casement he'd be entering in less than twenty-four hours to be with his one true love.

Tilly. Just the thought of her made his limbs go weak with longer.

With a notable exception, he amended, reflecting with pleasure on the fact that she was as eager in the bedroom department as he.

Not only did she lack self consciousness, her mind was sharp and her interests varied. What a wife she would make.

For a few pleasurable minutes he allowed his mind to wander these avenues in between contemplating the specifics of what he must do to effect their flight to Gretna Green, when a sharp rap sounded upon the drawing room door.

Expecting to see his valet on the threshold with confirmation of his post-chaise and four, he was surprised to see a young maid of all work looking flustered as she pulled a twist of paper from her apron pocket which she brandished before him.

"And who is this from?" he asked, as he dropped a coin into her grubby palm.

Perhaps too overawed to answer, the girl shrugged and hurried back towards the door.

"Stop!" he cried.

She turned.

"Did Miss Manners give this to you?" The message had clearly been written in haste and was unsigned.

The girl shook her head. "The mistress, Miss Grenville, give it to me, sir."

"Miss Grenville?" Henry frowned. He looked once more at the scrawl, then back at the girl. "When were you given this?"

She looked blank.

"Can you elaborate on the circumstances surrounding the writing of this note?"

The girl looked even more blank. "Alabrate?" She rubbed her nose with a grubby fist.

Henry reread the note, his agitation growing. Although he hadn't seen Tilly's handwriting, he was certain it must be from her. Tilly was in trouble and she needed Henry's help. She just had not stated the nature of the trouble, and her whereabouts.

"Can you tell me if you saw who wrote this note?" The sentence was unfinished. "Were other people about?"

"'Parently there were commotion at Miss Grenville's 'ouse early this mornin', sir." The girl's eyes brightened at the chance to relate what must be an unusual level of excitement at the old widow's residence. "Three persons, sir. From the aristocracy, sir. That's what Mrs Mawley, the housekeeper, told us downstairs. "Said there'd been a terrible robbery last night at Lady Lethbridge's ball and that's why these aristocratic persons knocked on Miss Grenville's door demandin' justice." She shook her head in wonder. "To think the thief were that young lady what reads to Miss Grenville. Stole thousands of pounds worth of jewels, she did, and might a' got away with it, too, if them folks weren't so quick on the scent. Well, that's wot Ben, the bootboy said, leastaways." She smiled. "If that'll be all, then, sir."

"Not yet! Wait!" Henry hurried to his writing desk and pulled out pen and paper. "Where is the young lady now?"

The girl shrugged.

"Is she still at Miss Grenville's townhouse?"

"Dunno, sir."

"Find out exactly where she is and I'll give you half a crown." Henry rose from his task. "Deliver this to Miss Tilly Manners and make sure you bring me back an answer. If you do that, I'll give you half a sovereign."

Her mouth fell open as she hurried forward to snatch the note. "I'll find her, sir. Don't you worry about that. No need to worry about a fing!"

But Henry was consumed with worry.

Again and again he returned to Tilly's note as he paced his chamber, wondering the best course of action.

"Lady Quamby has accused me of theft. Lady Wylie, too. It's untrue, Henry. I know who did it but—"

The note had ended there. There was nothing to indicate where he might find Tilly, or what the circumstances were behind the accusations she claimed had been levelled against her.

Just as shocking, though, was that Lady Quamby was an accuser.

Henry rapped his fingernails upon the windowsill as he strove for inspiration.

Someone wished to blacken Tilly's name.

Of course, there were a few people who did not consider Tilly a suitable bride for Henry. But would they go so far as to accuse her of theft?

He began to pace, raking his hand through his hair as his mind ran over the possibilities.

Henry knew his mother had been in Lady Quamby's ear. She'd accused Lady Quamby of failing to vet the young ladies who had attended her Instruction of Graceful Accomplishments. But had Henry's mother's pique been sufficient to prompt Lady Quamby to go so far as to frame Tilly for a crime she did not commit?

Not for one moment did Henry believe Tilly guilty of the charges against her.

He was confident Lady Quamby didn't believe it, either.

So what *had* prompted his mother's goddaughter, and Tilly's one-time benefactress, to turn against Tilly?

Hurrying back upstairs, calling for his valet, he dressed hastily while telling the man what to do in the event that a letter was delivered to him from the maid servant.

Then, shrugging on his outerwear and a low crowned beaver upon his head, he let himself out into the warm summer air.

IT TOOK ONLY ten minutes to cover the distance between his townhouse and Lord and Lady Quamby's Grosvenor Square address.

There he was shown into the drawing room and greeted with a surprising degree of care and concern by Lady Quamby herself, who looked remarkably well rested and serene. Her sister, Lady Fenton, was seated on a blue and gold settee speaking earnestly to a gentleman introduced as Mr Squigley, man of business to the magistrate, Sir Bradbury. The fellow's long neck and a bald pate gave him the look of a scavenging sea bird Henry fancied he'd seen up north.

In Dover, Tilly's birthplace. Or the place where she'd been claimed, and found a family, he reminded himself.

Up, where the cliffs gleamed white, and the sea hurled itself with unrelenting intensity onto jagged rocks.

Inhospitable territory where the local inhabitants had to be strong and tough to survive their harsh surroundings.

Tilly was a survivor. She'd grown from a foundling child into a confident, lively young woman despite the trials and tribulations nature had thrown at her.

She'd survive whatever was thrown at her now.

Only this time, she'd have Henry to watch her back and protect her from those who believed she had no right to what Henry was determined to give her.

And that included his name, he vowed grimly as he made his way from the threshold of the drawing room to the centre of the room where he now addressed Lady Quamby in brittle tones.

"I believe Miss Manners was taken from her residence this morning to answer charges of theft," he said, standing stiff and proud. Making it clear where his allegiance lay.

"Henry, I'm so sorry." It was Lady Fenton who rose and went to him. Her expression was sorrowful. She looked as if she believed the charge could be true.

"Miss Manners is not a thief." He stated it baldly, though he accepted the need for good manners and that too pugnacious a tone might injure her cause. "Where is she now, and how is her case to be judged?"

Lady Quamby now rose from her seat where she'd been

talking to Henry's own mama, he was shocked to note, and glided over to them. "Henry, I'm afraid Miss Manners was caught purloining a valuable emerald necklace. This morning it was discovered in her bedchamber."

Outrageous! But he did not say it. He stiffened, but kept his temper.

"Might I ask who made the accusation?"

Lady Quamby looked coy. "It doesn't matter and, indeed, it wasn't an accusation, it was only a suspicion, that she voiced." Her tone hardened. "Unfortunately, when Miss Manners' bedchamber was searched, the emerald necklace, together with a number of other missing items, was found."

Henry digested this in silence. "I still would like to know the identity of her accuser, Lady Quamby."

"It was Lady Wylie."

Henry turned to his mother, who had spoken. He made a derisive noise. "Lady Wylie has long held Tilly in dislike!"

"Perhaps because she always suspected the young woman was a thief," his mother returned calmly. "They hail from the same village. Lady Wylie has known Tilly Manners longer than you have. She'd know exactly the kind of person she is."

"Your logic does not follow, mama. Perhaps Lady Wylie has other reasons for disliking Tilly." Henry struggled to keep his tone even. "How do you suppose Tilly managed to steal an emerald necklace from around Lady Wylie's neck in the middle of a ball? It sounds as if Lady Wylie is prepared to go to enormous lengths to black Tilly's name and *that* is at the root of all this."

Mrs Garrick clicked her tongue, her eyes cold as she looked at her son who had moved to stand by the fireplace, opposite Lady Quamby, who looked considerably more fired up than she had a few minutes ago.

Though this was hardly surprising, Henry supposed, considering the new angle Henry had introduced to the drama.

Mrs Garrick huffed out a breath. "Henry, my boy, love is blind, and you have been completely taken in by this creature--"

Lady Quamby interrupted. "And Lady Wylie is not the only accuser."

Lady Fenton looked enquiringly at her sister. Lady Quamby's mouth was a censorious line.

"Who is this other accuser?" Henry felt like tarring him in feathers for even suggesting that Tilly could be anything other than as honest and pure as the driven snow.

Lady Quamby shook her head. "It doesn't matter. The fact is that Tilly Manners was found to be guilty. Stolen items were discovered in her bedchamber. Reassuringly, however, is the fact she can do no more harm, for she is being held by Sir Bradbury, the magistrate, and she will soon be conveyed somewhere more appropriate to one of her cunning." Her voice dropped to something between the husky purr Henry had heard her use on her latest friend and no doubt lover, Lord Ranulf, and the benevolent tone she'd used many times on Henry as a sop for his disappointment, mostly when reiterating why a match between Tilly and him was not possible. "Please understand, Henry, that we are all sympathetic to what you are feeling right now—"

"What else is she supposed to have stolen?" Henry interrupted.

Lady Quamby sighed, but his mother said in plaintive tones, "My dear boy, far too much! Those people who are missing items from last night's ball will convene here in an hour to lay claim to their property." Her voice quavered. "You may wish to absent yourself if it is so painful to accept the truth of the girl you once professed to love."

"I shall go nowhere." Though Henry's tone was stiff, his mind raced to find a way to exonerate his beloved. Tilly had not secreted that emerald necklace beneath her bed, but someone else had. And they had to be revealed. "Not only will I be here, but I would like Miss Manners to be present, also, to face her accusers." He looked at the three women and the gentleman.

His mother began to weep. An awkward silence crept over the rest of the company, broken by the sound of running footsteps in the passage.

Then the young maid of all work whom Henry had charged with delivering his note burst into the room, saying breathlessly, with an excitement that suggested she was hopeful of lavish recompense, "I got the information you wanted sir. I know where the lady is locked up and it's writ right here. That, and uvver fings she said was important you know."

CHAPTER 25

RIGHT WAS ON TILLY'S SIDE, BUT LADY WYLIE AND LORD RANULF were well connected, and Henry realised the power they wielded.

Seated in Lady Quamby's saloon as he waited for Tilly to arrive, Henry watched many he recognised from last night's ball file into the room.

Of course, they were not all there. Only a handful of guests had had jewellery purloined.

But a great many more people than those who were victims of the shocking crime were in attendance and it was very clear to Henry that the titillating factor was more in evidence than the sober desire to see justice done.

He'd been forced to leave Tilly with only an undertaking from Sir Bradbury that she would be brought to the proceedings.

Now, Madam Chambon was declaring in shrill tones that if she did not see her sapphire earrings again, then she'd personally push out the vessel to sea that would take Miss Manners to the colonies.

She was interrupted by Miss Snape, a bony, humourless

creature who suggested that the hangman's noose would be a more apt punishment.

It took all Henry's willpower not to vault over the settee and suggest to her, with his own bony hands about her neck, that a person was still considered innocent until guilty.

"Can you tell me," he now asked in a voice loud enough to cut into the low babble of outrage as everyone waited for the so-called prisoner, "why both Miss Manners' accusers are not here?"

"Lord Ranulf is confident that Sir Barnaby will see justice done." Lady Quamby sounded defensive before her tone softened. "The poor young man battled with his conscience before he drew attention to what he had seen, knowing, of course, the consequences." She cleared her throat, adding, "He was informed this morning that the stolen items were found in Miss Manners' bedchamber."

"Yet now he is not here?" Henry clarified.

"He has been called to the deathbed of a dear close relative. It has all been too much, these last twenty-four hours," muttered Lady Quamby as if her trials were so much greater than poor Tilly's.

More guests filed into Lady Quamby's saloon. The cluster of chairs and sofas, occupied by people in companionable groups, was supplemented by wooden chairs from the dining room which the servants set up against the wall. Of course, many were only in attendance for the circus-like nature of the event.

The fact that Tilly was supposedly behind it all was ludicrous. And yet, what could be said to exonerate her? Stolen property had been found in her bed chamber this very morning when three reputable personages had undertaken a thorough search.

Of course, she had not put it there.

But the man who claimed she had was not present. The man

who was Lady Quamby's lover. The man who had stolen before. First from Tilly, then from Lady Wylie.

And, even if she didn't know it, from Lady Quamby.

Heat washed over Henry, and he shifted, his head in his hands.

How could this information be brought into the proceedings in a way that was relevant?

Henry would soon be Lord Lomax, but right now he was plain Mr Garrick, who had fallen in love with the village girl who'd been accused of this terrible crime.

He swallowed past the lump in his throat and tried to order his thoughts. He must be quick to any opportunity to point out anomalies in the evidence. He couldn't make accusations that could not be borne out.

His desperation rose. Where was Tilly?

Lord Quamby fanned himself as he lounged on a settee next to his sister in law, Lady Fenton. He was sweating and looked old and uncomfortable. His beautiful wife looked as if she were hiding her distress beneath a carefully curated smile of sympathy, which she levelled at those who had lost property at the previous night's entertainment; and at Lord and Lady Lethbridge, who looked suitably aggrieved as they entered the room, and seating was found for them.

In front of the gathering, a low table was set with a silver serving plate covered with a dome. Near Henry, a group of ladies speculated in loud whispers as to what was concealed beneath.

"I lost a pearl necklace," said one, leaning in. "I barely slept all night. Indeed, I felt a tugging about my neck as I was preparing to step into the carriage, and now am consumed by the horror that she could have used a knife at my throat to gain satisfaction. But now the satisfaction will be mine to see my necklace revealed beneath that silver cover."

She pointed at the table while her friend added, "and the

satisfaction of seeing the lying, thieving imposter who so nearly got away with her crimes, get the sentence she deserves."

Henry kept his head in his hands. When Tilly finally got here, she'd be stepping into a room where everyone had already decided judgement upon her.

CHAPTER 26

TILLY TRAVELLED FROM SIR BRADBURY'S RESIDENCE WITH HER face pressed to the window of the carriage in which she'd been despatched.

It might be the last time she beheld anything other than a convict ship, she reflected, for the monetary value of all that had been found in her room was in the thousands of pounds.

Indeed, it may even be the noose for her.

When the carriage came to a stop outside Lord Quamby's townhouse and she stepped into the street, she was astonished to see Matilda hurrying along in the company, of all people, handsome Mr Fortescue. Two older women clung to each arm, and one of these was Miss Grenville, who was clearly doing her best to keep up with his determined stride.

"Matilda, I don't think you should be here," Tilly whispered as the lackey who had just assisted her out of the carriage, conversed in a hurried undertone with another gentleman.

Tilly sent a baleful look at her wrist, for the lackey had kept firm hold of her. Then she fixed Matilda with an imploring look. "Don't come inside. There will be a lot of uncomfortable questions, including the fact that your jewellery case was also

202

found in my chamber." She flicked a look at Mr Fortescue, who was currently being addressed by his mama and Miss Grenville, then lowered her voice. "If I'm to be accused of all the rest, I might as well save you the embarrassment of explaining why your jewellery was not with you."

Matilda looked uncharacteristically determined. "Lady Wylie tried to keep me away, which is all the more reason for me to come. She all but locked me in the house but when I opened the window to call out to Mr Fortescue whom I saw in the street below, passing by with his mama, he prevailed upon the servant to unlock my door, saying Lady Wylie had requested it. He said what was needed to release me, and I will say whatever I need to if it'll help you, Tilly. Even if it brings shame to me." She looked more shaken than Tilly had seen her.

The lackey, having ended his conversation without having loosened his grip on Tilly's wrist, now turned and, nodding at Mr Fortescue and his little entourage, finished with a glower at Tilly.

"Come along, my girl," he said with a nod at Lord Quamby's townhouse, "It's time to go in."

Tilly had never been so terrified in her life but as they reached the drawing room, Mr Fortescue leaned across his mama and, with a smile—accompanied by fierce nodding from Miss Grenville—said to her, "The truth will prevail, Miss Manners. I do not for a moment believe you are guilty, and neither will anyone else when this little charade is at an end."

At least, that's what Tilly believed he said, for a great murmuring filled her ears as the double doors were opened, cutting off the end of his sentence; and Tilly was led to a spindly yellow upholstered chair a little to the right of a low table upon which the stolen items would be revealed, she overheard, in order that those who had lost property the previous night could state their claim.

Before, no doubt, the accused would be summarily despatched to a prison cell.

The one bright spot was that Henry was near the front, his smile warm and encouraging.

Even if this was the last sight she had of him, the fact that he believed in her would sustain her to the end.

HENRY HOPED the look he sent Tilly would be enough for her to hold her nerve. Tearful denials would do her no good; but Tilly was sharp as a whip and bold as a tiger.

What a wife she was going to make, he thought as Sir Bradbury rose to address the gathering.

"I begin these painful proceedings with a short summation of the character of the accused—"

"Good lord, that has no bearing on the matter!" Henry exclaimed, rising.

"Sit down, sir," Sir Bradbury instructed sharply. "Or I shall ask you to leave."

Reluctantly Henry lowered himself back into his seat, glowering at the magistrate who went on in his reedy, monotonous voice, "The accused, known to many here as Tilly Manners, is in fact nameless. That is, she has no known blood relatives. No mother, no father. Only two gypsy sisters who found her wandering, a foundling child, and took her into their home—"

"They're not gypsies!" Tilly interjected before she was silenced by a look from Henry. She realised she should save her interruptions for when they were important.

Sir Bradbury ignored her. "Some weeks ago, she brazenly insinuated herself into Lady Quamby's good offices, taking advantage of her kindness by pretending to be a cousin of a young lady—another kind young lady who was also deceived."

A general murmur of disapproval issued from the more than

three dozen people who'd fixed their gazes upon Tilly. Some assessed her as if she were some oddity in a circus; others with greater horror, as if she were some evil manipulator.

"Mr Garrick, here, asks what bearing this has on the matter before us." Sir Bradbury's yellow teeth gleamed. "It is all about motive. A young person who is skilled at impersonating her betters may start with simple friendship. But when she is confronted by riches she can never possess, why, she cannot help herself."

Ignoring Henry's vocal disapproval and the general hubbub this occasioned, Sir Bradbury made a sweeping gesture with his arm towards the table.

"Let me say that the purpose of today's gathering is not to pass judgement on Tilly, whose family name we do not know, which is why I do not address her by any other name. No, judgement will be passed in a court of law. The purpose today is for you good people to bolster the unassailable case against her by claiming the property she has stolen from you." He nodded to a hovering footman who stepped forward and, with gloved hands, gripped the handle of the silver lid.

Tilly felt her breath disappear in a whoosh as the cover was raised and placed to one side. A gasp reverberated about the room and people stood and craned their necks. She knew what they were thinking: Who would have thought one seemingly harmless girl could be so dangerous?

And how had she got to this point? An innocent swapping of places so that Matilda could win the affections of Mr Griggs who was not even here.

Ah, yes, but of course he was, for he was not the kind of man to miss out on sport like this. He had found Matilda and was seated close beside her.

"My emerald necklace!" It was Lady Wylie who spoke first, moving regally across to the table to raise her very costly piece of jewellery, which she brandished with satisfaction in front of her husband, Tilly noted.

He did not smile, she also noted, but rather his lip curled as his wife prepared to take her seat beside him.

But she hesitated and pointed at Tilly, adding for good measure, "See there the person who stole it last night! For it was found under her bed this morning!"

Sir Bradbury cut into the rumble of general indignation. "Ladies and gentlemen, silence, if you please. For those who do not know, everything you see on this table was, this morning, retrieved from beneath this young lady's bed. Look at her!" The finger he stabbed in Tilly's direction was accompanied by a baleful glower. "See how adept she is at deception for my first instinct is to call her a lady. That is, after all, how she has become used to being addressed during the course of her wicked deception. For it is on that basis she is here: shameful deception, for she is nothing but a nameless guttersnipe brought up by gypsies who found her wandering and abandoned above the white cliffs of Dover."

The crowd tutted their disapproval.

"To that that all this time Miss Manners really *was* a gypsy?" Tilly heard one venerable widow utter in shocked tones.

Henry leapt up. "Miss Manners is not a gypsy. She is a young woman of moral integrity who has been falsely accused and I intend to make her my wife when her name is cleared—"

"Henry, no!" his mother begged in distress, while a tall gentleman, coming forward to claim his time piece, challenged him as he raised his lost property, saying with clear disgust, "Moral integrity? When she stole this from me last night?" before he pointed an accusing finger at Tilly.

Tilly felt like shrivelling up. She'd welcomed the opportunity to declare her innocence, but so many cold, hard faces made her realise the impossibility of her hopes.

She *was* an imposter, just as Sir Bradbury had claimed. And the public liked to be deceived even less than they liked to be fleeced of their valuables.

The fact was that the more that was said, the more was stacked up against her.

Henry was here to champion her, but his was a lone voice in the room.

She glanced at Matilda, who looked scared and small, seated beside Mr Griggs, whose thigh was wedged against hers, his expression full of moral rectitude as he patted her hand.

Tilly felt a mix of regret and resignation overlaid by an attempt at feeling happy for her friend. Matilda was nothing if not determined. And her determination had won her the man of *her* heart, at least. Even if Tilly thought him a bounder.

"And those are my earrings," Lady Quamby said crisply, coming forward to raise one diamond and pearl earring before the company.

"And you weren't even wearing them last night!" Lady Fenton interjected, prompting someone else to cry out, "Why, the girl must have been thieving long before this. To think that this is the way she repays you after all the opportunities you gave her, Lady Quamby."

Tilly gazed at the beautiful bauble she'd supposedly purloined. She'd seen Lady Fenton wear these earrings a few times at Quamby House near Bath. No doubt there would be more missing items, dating back to this time, for which she'd be blamed.

She glanced up and noted the furrow between Lady Quamby's eyes as her husband asked, "And where is the other?"

Of course, all eyes turned to Tilly, and someone said, "Has the girl nothing to say for herself? Stand up, girl! Where is my ruby choker? I cannot see it on the table but it most definitely went missing last night."

"And where is my diamond pin? It's not there, either," someone else interjected, causing the room to erupt into a cacophony of anger and accusation which had Sir Bradbury shouting for silence.

"We shall proceed with matters in an orderly way. Of importance, naturally, is that missing property is reunited with its owner. And testimony from the young person accused will be taken once she is removed from here, as we follow lawful procedure."

"Why not let her speak for herself in front of us all here today?" Henry said, standing, while his mother tugged at his coattails in a futile attempt to quieten him. "Would it not be more satisfactory to all here to learn how indeed this supposedly ingenious creature, the hapless—in my eyes—Miss Manners, managed to separate you all from your valuables, last night, with no one the wiser? I consider that an incredible achievement, yet no one has thought to wonder how it was even possible?"

Sir Bradbury waved him aside, bending to pick up a bracelet set with lapis lazuli. "We shall endeavour to ensure that everything here is accounted for. In this room are a great many people but only a few items on the table, as you can see. I suspect Miss Manners has an accomplice, but we will get to the bottom of that. Now, does someone claim this?" He held aloft an emerald bracelet which was claimed with a squeak of indignation by a hump-backed dowager.

"And this?" Now a thin gold chain and cross were held up. "Not an item of value, but thieves do not distinguish," said Sir Bradbury.

"It is mine."

Matilda stood. The girl's eyes were downcast and her cheeks flamed. "But it was I who put it in Miss Manners' bedchamber." She raised her head and sent a defiant look about the room. "She did not take the chain or any of my jewellery which you see there."

Mr Griggs looked scandalised as he put a hand on Matilda's wrist and exhorted her to sit down.

Ignoring him, Matilda pointed to the table. "Most of what you see there is mine. Not of great value, but mine nevertheless, for I had my jewel box and—" she struggled to get the words out — "a few other belongings in Tilly's room last night." Perceiving how her words might be misinterpreted, she added, quickly, "I didn't put them there to apportion blame, but because of a previous... arrangement." She glanced at Mr Griggs, who looked away.

Tilly wondered if he would say anything. He'd not wish to be revealed as a bounder on the cusp of whisking away an heiress six months before she came into her inheritance.

Sir Bradbury indicated for Matilda to resume her seat, but, despite looking even more frightened, she ignored him. She cleared her voice and tried to raise her voice. "Miss Manners is staying in the townhouse beside mine. There's an underground passageway that connects the two residences, and I've used it a couple of times to see my friend when—" she glanced at Lady Wylie, then added— "because I'd been previously forbidden by my chaperone to see her since she dislikes her excessively."

Lady Wylie's nostrils flared, and she said crisply, "A precaution you'd have been wise to have adhered to." She tried to say more, no doubt to deflect Matilda, who stood her ground and went on, stoically, "I was therefore surprised when Lady Wylie invited Miss Manners to accompany us to last night's ball. Her kindness was unprecedented, and Miss Manners and I danced all three sets until we were taken home early, so I don't know how Tilly could have taken all the things she's supposed to have."

Henry waited, stiff and poised, for Sir Bradbury to ask the obvious question.

What else had Miss Harcourt seen, both at the ball, and when she deposited her belongings? And why had she deposited her belongings?

Clearly the girl had something to offer this investigation yet Sir Bradbury had painted Tilly as a thief purely on account of the circumstantial evidence that lay before them: that the discovery in Tilly's room of the jewellery therefore made her guilty.

When Sir Bradbury now allowed Lady Wylie to expound further on her low assessment of his beloved, he could bear it no longer. Miss Harcourt had resumed her seat, clearly overcome by the nerves occasioned by pubic scrutiny and the acceptance that she would not be allowed to continue, but Henry leapt to his feet and asked her directly, "So, Miss Harcourt, if you came home with Miss Manners, how do you suppose she could have carried off so many items of value without you noticing?"

"It would seem, now, that only a handful of valuables were purloined by Miss Manners," remarked Sir Bradbury triumphantly. "If Miss Harcourt says that many of these items are hers, then Miss Manners' reticule could easily have held the rest. Those remaining items that are missing have clearly been handed on to an accomplice. Rest assured, that person will also be brought to justice," he added in response to the mutterings of the crowd.

"Miss Harcourt, did you see Miss Manners take anything?" Henry called out, trying to be heard above the growing noises of discontent.

She shook her head as she sent Henry a look of desperation. When she glanced at Mr Griggs, he looked away.

"What time did you leave your possessions in her room and did you see anything else?" Again this was from Henry, which earned a hearty complaint from Sir Bradbury that he was not the one investigating the matter.

"Then do your job and ask the questions you should be asking," Henry said angrily.

Matilda rose quickly to her feet once more. "Miss Manners said she was tired and not to come to see her before ten the next morning. Which is, of course today. But I was too excited after I couldn't sleep, and I wanted to speak to her, so I made my way over using the underground tunnel, to her room which was, of course, unlocked, as there is no lock on the door."

"Did the two of you speak?" Sir Bradbury asked.

"No. Miss Manners was fast asleep, and I decided not to disturb her, but merely to leave my bag of possessions under her bed."

"And why should you wish to do that, Miss Manners?"

"Does that have any bearing on the matter?" asked Mr Griggs in such sharp and angry tones that everyone in the room looked at him in surprise.

"Did you notice anything unusual, Miss Harcourt?" Henry called out.

She nodded. "The catch of the casement was undone, and it was rattling rather loudly. I was sure it would have woken Miss Manners, but it seemed she was in a very deep sleep. So I went across the room to close it, and I found this." She raised a marker in the shape of a fish."

"A lottery ticket. What of it, Miss Harcourt?" It was Lady Wylie. Her tone was strained, yet there seemed a clear attempt to sound bored and dismissive.

"It had been dropped on the windowsill. It's a gaming counter made of mother-of-pearl. See how unusual it is?" Matilda raised it high. "Miss Manners does not play at quadrille, and I'm sure that this belongs to someone who has a special set of fish markers."

"Stolen, no doubt, by the young lady in question," Sir Bradbury said.

"But there were no card games played at last night's ball,"

said Henry. "Miss Harcourt, can you hold it up again and show everyone so they might see to whom it belongs? It's very unusual."

"Why, it's one of the fish you had made for Ranulf!" Lady Fenton exclaimed, rising and holding her hand out. "See, Antoinette! It belongs to Ranulf, without doubt. Where did you say he'd gone?"

Henry looked at Lady Quamby, who blushed and turned away, saying indistinctly, "As I said, he's had to leave on some urgent business."

Henry raised his voice. "Was it not Lord Ranulf who claimed in the early hours of this morning that he'd seen Miss Manners slip a jewelled comb from Lady Huntingdon's coiffure without that lady noticing?" Henry sent an enquiring look about the room. "I would have thought he should be here. If only to claim *his* gaming counter," he added in tones of disgust before asking, "Why do you suppose it was found on Miss Manners' window sill? Would the girl steal only one gaming counter? Pretty, of course, but without value unless she had the whole set. I find that very perplexing."

A few murmurs went about the room. Henry studied Lady Quamby. She was known to be indiscreet, however, she clearly was not about to reveal any secrets relating to her and Lord Ranulf for she now removed another item from the silver tray and asked, "Does this belong to anyone?" as she held up a brooch made of carved wood. "Very pretty but not valuable, though the artistry is commendable. I'm sure it's an item of great sentimentality. Thieves do not distinguish."

"Why Millicent, that's yours!" came a robust female voice.

Tilly couldn't see the item, but a surge of gratitude swept through her as Matilda, who was closest to the item, cried out, "No, it's not. It's Tilly's. I mean, it belongs to Miss Manners." For Matilda was being as true a friend as Tilly could have wished for.

To Tilly's surprise, the response to Matilda's words was surprisingly outraged. "With due respect, that belongs to Millicent, my daughter. And while it is true, the brooch has little monetary value, it was painted by her grandmother. Its loss would be greatly lamented."

Tilly tried to see the brooch that was being described. She could not, but she saw the determination on the face of the thin-faced, grey-haired woman dressed in emerald green silk, speaking. She was seated beside a gentleman with sumptuous side whiskers; presumably her husband, for his hand was outstretched, and he was now laying claim to the item which came into view only now that Lady Quamby had reseated herself.

This time, the outrage belonged to Tilly. "It's mine!" she cried indignantly, for this was one possession she was not going to see wrongly attributed to thievery. "I've had it my whole life. Please, give it back to me, for it is not yours, I assure you!"

"Miss Manners, a thief has no right—" Sir Bradbury said in sonorous tones.

"But it *is* mine! It's all I have left!" she cried.

"Suspend the drama, if you would," said Sir Bradbury, more angrily this time.

The injustice Tilly had already suffered had left her bruised and confused. But seeing her most prized possession claimed because some stranger fancied the pretty painted flowers was more than she could bear.

"Give it back!" she cried, leaping once more to her feet. "You have no right to take what is not yours. I am not a thief, but even if you believe I was, it doesn't make it right to steal from me!"

The woman in emerald clearly took umbrage at Tilly's tone, for she now rose and, her cheeks flaming, cried, "Hold your tongue, girl! Have you no shame!"

Her daughter—for the slender dark-haired young woman

beside her bore a strong family resemblance—put out her hand and gripped her mother's sleeve. "Tell her it's mine, mother!"

Tilly could not believe it. Tears welled in her eyes. She'd have given up all the diamonds and rubies in the world if she could only have kept the wooden brooch.

She caught Matilda's eye, and to her surprise, the girl rose once more. Matilda looked overawed, but her voice, though it wavered, was firm. "My friend is not a thief. She's been wearing that brooch for as long as I've known her—more than twelve years! It's all she has left of her old life. I know that for a fact! And it was on her wash stand last night when I was in her room, because that's where she always puts it when she's not wearing it, though she wears it every day. I do the same, for, like me, Miss Manners is an orphan, and it's comforting to wear the only keepsake one has from one's mother. Please, give it back to her."

"Now, does anyone else—" Sir Bradbury began to speak over Matilda, but the trio who had tried to steal Tilly's brooch and who had their heads together, murmuring in growing agitation —and Tilly didn't care but she was not surrendering her brooch to them—suddenly broke apart.

"We have the other brooch here!" The gentleman stood. He looked stern with his beetling brows knitted together, his iron grey hair brushed back from a receding hairline. "Now there are two. And they are identical."

He was holding them out, and those around him were sending curious glances amongst each other, for the items were made of carved wood and painted as a flower. Not valuable at all, though the carving was delicate and expert.

"If you care to look, my name is on the back," said Tilly.

"Matilda?" The woman took a step forward. Her voice sounded uncertain for the first time.

"That's my name," interrupted Matilda, looking confused. "But it's Tilly's brooch. She told me that the first time we met."

"When you first met? Where?"

"We're from Elham, a village in Dover. Well, I was born there. Tilly doesn't know where she was born."

There was a flurry of whispered conversation between the elderly pair in consultation with their tall, dark-haired daughter.

Then the gentleman pushed back his shoulders. He seemed angry until Tilly realised his emotion stemmed from something else. "Matilda," he repeated, and Matilda answered obediently, "Yes, sir? I'm Miss Matilda Harcourt."

He frowned at her. "Yes, yes, I remember the name. I have, in fact, met you before, Miss Harcourt. When you were just a child of four. You would not remember me and, besides, you had just come through a terrible ordeal."

Matilda's eyes widened. "My parents died when I was four. A bridge collapsed and their carriage was washed into the river."

The woman took up position beside her husband, and so did the younger woman. Tilly heard whispers that she was Lady Huntingdon, and she glanced quickly at Henry. Hadn't he mentioned that Lady Huntingdon had been suggested as a potential bride?

Henry was confused. Where was this questioning going?

He didn't know what to say, but listened as the trio took control of the room. Sir Bradbury also looked confused, but clearly he was not going to tell his social superiors to be silent when, in fact, this was not a court of law.

The older woman spoke. "Miss Harcourt, you lost your parents in the same accident that claimed our daughter," she said. "Forgive me, I am Lady Wells. And please indulge me for just a few minutes." She flicked a covert glance at Tilly, pressed her lips together, then turned back to Tilly's friend. "When we searched in the days and weeks following the accident, we were directed to you. We thought perhaps our Matilda had been swept downstream, so when we heard there was a child called Matilda associated with the terrible storm that night we held out such great hopes."

"But I was not in the carriage with my parents," said Matilda. "I was with my uncle, who is now my guardian." She lowered her eyes. "For my parents drowned when the carriage sunk to the bottom of the river."

Tilly noticed how quiet the room was as everyone listened to the exchange. A strange feeling had entered her bones. She couldn't identify it. It wasn't fear; it wasn't hope; it wasn't disbelief.

And yet it was all these things, and more.

"Just as we had to accept that our daughter was also drowned when the mail coach sank," said Lady Wells. Her shoulders slumped. "When we met you, Miss Manners, we realised that the Matilda for whom we had held out such hope of finding was...." She hesitated. "Not our daughter." She turned to look at her husband and the young woman who obviously was her daughter. "So we returned home to Somerset, and we had a memorial to our lost Matilda who..." She seemed to be puzzling something out as she spoke. Silence reined. Everyone was quiet. It seemed a moment of great importance. More importance than the theft.

"I didn't steal the brooch." Tilly spoke softly, though her words sounded loud in the silence.

The noise of everyone turning to look at her was muffled and muted. Tilly shook her head. She remained standing. "My sisters—the women I call my sisters, though they are not, really —told me I was wearing the brooch when they found me wandering near the forest. They were going to take me to a foundling home, but then decided to keep me, for I was good with my hands, and they needed small, nimble hands for their finer piece work. They said Matilda was a name for a lady but that Tilly was more appropriate for the kinds of people they were."

Tilly frowned at the trio. They seemed so strange and remote.

Slowly, Lady Wells turned from Matilda to face Tilly. With heavy, cumbersome footsteps for a woman so slender and of such fragile appearance, she made her way out from the row of chairs where she'd been seated. Her husband and daughter followed her.

None of them hurried, and Tilly felt the oddest sensation in her breast: fear when it should have been hope.

"Millicent, please stand beside Miss... Manners," commanded Lord Wells.

Obediently, Lady Huntingdon did as directed. Like Tilly, she was tall, her hair as black as a raven's wing, her skin a perfect translucent white.

And her nose... It was the same-shaped patrician proboscis that Tilly's had been laughingly described.

And then the whole room erupted with a collective gasp.

CHAPTER 27

 behind her, Tilly gazed at the crowd who were here to witness the most important event of her life.

Not her public hanging, though for a tense few hours four weeks earlier this had seemed a distinct possibility.

She'd even escaped the lesser sentence of deportation to the colonies.

For, of course, she'd been exonerated regarding the thefts. It had soon become clear that Lord Ranulf had made false claims against Tilly in order to buy himself time to decamp to the Continent with a great number of valuable pieces he'd stolen from those attending Lady Lethbridge's ball.

And an even greater quantity of jewels he'd stolen from Lady Quamby.

But that seemed of minor importance, now.

This was Tilly's wedding day, and she had just wed the kindest, most loyal and noble man in existence. Henry was standing beside her now, surreptitiously squeezing her hand as he accepted the well wishes that rained down upon them.

Many of these included people who had once filed into Lady Quamby's drawing room to see her vilified as a thief.

That had conveniently been forgotten, it seemed.

"Lady Lomax, you are a vision to behold." It was Lord Quamby, hobbling towards her over the uneven cobbles, his eyes rheumy with sentiment as he gripped her hand.

Lady Lomax. Yes, that's who she was. Not just plain Mrs Garrick. She was a countess.

Nor had she been plain Miss Tilly Manners prior to that, either.

As the daughter of the Earl of Wells, she'd been Lady Matilda for the few short weeks between the revelation of her real identity and her recent marriage.

Tilly's newly discovered aunt joined them. Tall and thin, like her sister, Lady Wells, but more demonstrative, she embraced her niece as if she'd known her all her life. "A vision wearing the same veil your mother wore for her wedding day." Reverently, she touched the Brussels lace that fell delicately from Tilly's headpiece. "Millicent wore it, too. I wish you could have seen her. She was a beauty. Like you."

Tilly wished she could have seen it. She wished she could have known her real family.

But would she have changed anything in her past considering it all led to this? Marriage with Henry?

No. She would not.

"Darling, are you ready for more?"

Henry, having dispensed with pleasantries with the guests to his right, patted Tilly's hand, signalling that there were others waiting to congratulate them, as her aunt moved away.

And indeed, there was Matilda, looking more radiant than Tilly had seen her, clinging to Mr Fortescue's arm. Her spoiled, dramatic, manipulative and ultimately loyal-to-the-end friend threw out her arms in a gesture of rapturous approval. "You will go down in history as England's most beautiful bride until it's my turn," she said. "Don't you think so, Max?"

Max Fortescue nodded. It was he who had exposed Mr Griggs as the scoundrel he was. A liar and a cheat, who had been prepared to go to any lengths to wed a rich wife to get his creditors off his back.

It was also Mr Fortescue who had rescued Matilda from her embarrassment following the shameful revelation that she'd been planning to elope with the worthless Mr Griggs.

A less honourable gentleman than Mr Fortescue might have quietly withdrawn his interest in Matilda, which had become obvious at Lady Lethbridge's ball and during the investigation into the subsequent theft.

Instead, he'd become Matilda's greatest champion.

By the time he'd asked Matilda to become his wife, Tilly had been able to reassure Matilda that her indiscretion with Mr Griggs would have no consequences.

Everyone made mistakes, and while Tilly had long accepted that in the society in which they lived, it was usually the women who paid for them, she felt she had the advantage for the knowledge she'd acquired during her strange upbringing.

Now, Matilda was looking happier than Tilly had seen her. For being wanted and loved had always been the goal of her orphaned friend.

Tilly, too, had found love. Enduring love, she was sure of it.

Henry was her rock and her greatest ally. He'd been determined to marry her, despite her origins, and then he'd navigated Sir Bradbury's course of questioning so that the truth of Tilly's innocence—and then her true origins—had been made clear.

And in such public fashion.

Less happily, Lady Wylie's reputation had taken a battering, yet of course, here she was on the sidelines of the well wishers. Perhaps it was her husband, standing stony faced sentinel beside her, who was behind her muttered congratulations, for

Tilly fancied he took a morose pleasure in seeing his wife all but prostrate herself before Tilly.

"I wish you all the happiness you deserve, Lady Lomax." Lady Wylie, nodded, adding stiffly, "And I am glad to have played my part in seeing you find your rightful place in society."

Tilly smiled. It was true, of course. Had Lady Wylie not used Tilly as a pawn to deflect attention from her own misdemeanours, then Tilly might, at this moment, have been in ignominious hiding on the continent with Henry while waiting for the scandal over their elopement to subside.

She would have been just as happy with Henry, regardless of under what circumstances she'd married him, but now her elevated status made her his equal in the eyes of the world.

And how much better that was for both of them.

Now that Tilly had been reunited with her family, she was hopeful she would come to love them.

They had clearly been distraught to have lost her all those years ago, but they were reserved people who found it as difficult as Tilly to breach the great divide.

They were also good people who had shown kindness, rather than hostility, to Yasmin and Zena; and in fact Millicent was talking now to Tilly's adoptive sisters, who added a rebellious splash of colour to the company.

"I am glad, too, Lady Wylie," said Tilly graciously, even as she wondered how far Lady Wylie would have gone to have seen Tilly's reputation destroyed in order to protect her own.

Would she have turned a blind eye if Tilly had been sentenced to deportation? Or worse?

Lady Wylie's desperation over being blackmailed by Ranulf seemed to have unhinged her at the time. When he'd threatened to reveal their previous affair, only her complicity in helping him to plant the jewels he had stolen, in Tilly's bedchamber, would satisfy him.

He'd left the ball early in order to climb the tree outside Tilly's room, and then place the items under her bed.

Lady Wylie had been in the vanguard of declaring Tilly's guilt.

Tilly reminded herself to let bygones by bygones. After all, Tilly had nothing now of which to complain. And she was considerably happier than Lady Wylie.

She waited for Lady Wylie's reply which was cut short by a shout of laughter from Henry's friend a little distance away, which had everyone turning in his direction. Lady Quamby, who was helping her husband navigate the cobblestones, looked up at the sound of her name as she joined them.

"Oh, my dear Freddy, do say that again," Henry implored, his expression one of the greatest merriment as he ushered his friend into their circle.

Freddy was happy to oblige. "Of course it may not be true, but then I do have it on good authority that a gentleman with raven locks, answering to the description of Lord Ranulf, but calling himself Lord Babidge, was, just yesterday, in Chester, challenged to a duel by the cuckolded husband of the fair lady whose charms he'd been enjoying."

"It sounds like Ranulf," Tilly said with a nod, causing the little group consisting of both blood and adoptive relatives, to look at her in surprise, as if it were remarkable she should speak with such lack of shame.

"I knew Ranulf long before anyone else did," Tilly told them comfortably. "He stole from me when I was not yet eighteen, and although I tried to tell Lady Wylie and Lady Quamby that he was not the man he claimed to be, I was, I daresay, beneath anyone's notice at the time. "And," she added, "a gentleman with a handsome face and fine physique is always more inclined to be believed than a girl of unknown lineage. Those were, in fact, almost the very words Ranulf used when he forced me to dance with him at Lady Lethbridge's not long before he committed the thefts for which he blamed me, then disappeared."

"Well, from all accounts, his face is as fine but his physique has taken a battering," said Freddy. Raking back his sandy hair with a smile for the gathered company, he gave a chuckle.

Tilly noticed the tenseness on Lady Wylie's face, and the way Lady Quamby pressed together her own lips. To her credit, she was not so ashamed that she couldn't ask after the welfare of a man she cared for. "Ranulf might be a thief but he was a fighter, and good with his fists," she said. "And his hands."

"But not with a sword, it would seem," said Freddy.

Ranulf used to think he was capable of anything, thought Tilly. Though he might never have held a sword other than one he'd have stolen, he was from the gutter and his weapon of choice were his fists.

"He had the chance to withdraw, but declared he was up to anything; for my lady's husband was short of stature, with perhaps a visage that suggested to Lord Ranulf a weakness he could exploit."

"Oh, tell me he won't die!" Lady Quamby fixed an appealing look on her husband. "I know he stole from me, but you mustn't be cross with me for being upset, Quamby. Ranulf was vastly entertaining. And skilled."

She was clearly relieved when Lord Quamby appeared not to mind, and even more so when Freddy reassured her that this man who now called himself Lord Babidge had lost his wager. The supposed villain, Ranulf, was not dead and no longer in danger of dying.

"And I can happily add that no gentleman need ever fear being cuckolded by the man again thanks to a clean cut with what I believe its original owner referred to as his Sword of Spiritual Justice. Only in this case, I'd have called it a sword of Poetic Justice."

"Dear Lord, you don't mean—" Lady Quamby began.

Freddy looked grave. "He lost a lot of blood but has recovered his strength though it was feared he would expire. Sadly, however, the loss of his manhood is permanent."

"Matilda, there you are!" The voice bearing down on them broke up the party. Tilly noticed Lady Quamby and Lady Wylie looked pale and shaken, and she only turned her head in the direction of Lady Wells' voice when she realised it was she who was being addressed and not her friend.

"Yes, my dear, I'm speaking to you. And please forgive me, but for the last sixteen years I have called you my poor lost Matilda in my mind." Her mother took both her hands in her own and smiled. "I'm afraid it's too late to start calling you Tilly now."

The sun chose that moment to pop out from behind a cloud and while Lady Wells' grey hairs and age spots were shown in greater clarity, so too was the real love and kindness and relief in her eyes as she was flanked by her husband and daughter—Tilly's sister.

"I never thought I'd live to see this day," said Lord Wells, gruffly.

"And I never thought I'd have a sister again," said Millicent. She smiled at Henry before returning her gaze to Tilly's. "When you're back from your wedding tour, I hope you'll let me bore you with reminiscences of how we used to play together when you were four and I was eight."

Tilly had vague memories of such togetherness. It was something she'd held dear to her heart, and to see her own flesh and blood before her, looking at her with such pride, brought the tears to her eyes.

"I can't tell you how much I look forward to that," she said, with another glance at Henry whose mama was now beside him and smiling with similar joy.

"It does a mother's heart proud to see her son looking so content with his lot in life." Mrs Garrick touched Tilly's cheek a moment, before transferring her gaze to her son. "I always knew darling Tilly was the perfect bride for you."

THE END

If you enjoyed Tilly and Henry's story, why not read *The Accidental Elopement*, a friends to lovers, second-chance romance? It's book 4. Or, start at the beginning with racy Regency romp, *Rake's Honour*!

Would you like to know when I have new releases as well as get the romantic start to my Regency-set 'Dynasty'-inspired *Daughters of Sin* series?

I'll also send you a curated selection of free and discounted books from my fellow historical romance authors.

Get a FREE book when you sign up to my Newsletter.
Visit www.beverleyoakley.com

Book 3 - The Wedding Wager

A lonely young woman's bid to be reunited with her long-lost love child seems doomed after her friends' matchmaking attempts go awry.

When Miss Eliza Montrose's extraordinary bravery wins her the respect of matchmaking queens Fanny and Antoinette Brightwell, the sisters and their bumbling brother hatch a plan to find a worthier suitor for the young woman they'd initially disliked.

Rufus Patmore, a kind honorable gentleman with a love of horses and a soft spot for damsels in distress, is the ideal candidate when he inadvertently reveals his true feelings for Eliza.

But Eliza has her own reasons for agreeing to marry the Brightwells' selfish, self-absorbed cousin, George Bramley. Reasons that have nothing to do with love! If it's the only way to be reunited with the love child she was forced to give up after a youthful indiscretion, Eliza will marry anyone!

Unfortunately, while the Brightwell siblings have acted with the best of intentions, fixing a horse race that was supposed to bring joy and happiness to two deserving, star-crossed lovers has unfortunate consequences.

Now, being able to follow her heart comes at an unexpected price. A price that Eliza might not be able to pay.

What the Readers say:

"This was almost like reading a different version of pride and prejudice. Fabulous read. I love this author's work and this book definitely did not disappoint." ~ **Goodreads reader**

"A well written romance, with underlying suspense, Devil's Run (renamed The Wedding Wager) highlights the double standards, judgmental attitudes and abuse that many women were faced with in the Regency era." ~ **Kindle reader**

"Very much enjoyed this read from this author. Great plot and characters. Some tears for those who are sensitive but great enjoyment at the end." ~ **Goodreads reader**

"Written after the stye of Jane Austen, Ms Oakley brings out the quirkiness of country gentry and difficulties facing women of the times." ~ **Kindle reader**

Buy or read for FREE in Kindle Unlimited.

Other books in the series are:

The Honourable Fortune Hunter
Widowed Sebastian Wells has spent a year searching tire-

lessly for the girl he was forced to give up after honour required him to wed another.

When he discovers Venetia working as a lowly companion to the exacting Dowager Duchess Lady Indigo at a Christmas house party he's attending, their secret rendezvous turns scorching.

But Sebastian's hostesses, the scandalous Brightwell sisters, have paired him up with a lively, golden-haired debutante they believe will be his perfect match. And this young lady is determined to make everyone believe the lie.

Will honour once again compel Sebastian to act against the desires of his heart?

Buy or Read for Free in Kindle Unlimited

The Courtship Caper

Widowed Sebastian Wells has spent a year searching tirelessly for the girl he was forced to give up after honour required him to wed another.

When he discovers Venetia working as a lowly companion to the exacting Dowager Duchess Lady Indigo at a Christmas house party he's attending, their secret rendezvous turns scorching.

But Sebastian's hostesses, the scandalous Brightwell sisters, have paired him up with a lively, golden-haired debutante they believe will be his perfect match. And this young lady is determined to make everyone believe the lie.

Will honour once again compel Sebastian to act against the desires of his heart?

Read The Courtship Caper, free, in Kindle Unlimited

The Wilful Widow

This sweet novella takes us back to Katherine, Jack and George's childhood days.

However, this time, they're the matchmakers for a beautiful young widow who is about to embark upon a fifth marriage.

Unlike her, they know exactly whom she should be marrying!

Read The Wilful Widow FREE in KU

Or read the entire series in two box sets:

You can also read the books in this series in Kindle Unlimited.

Books 1-3
Books 4-7

HISTORICAL HARLOTS! PRIZES & LOTS OF FUN!

Hey everyone,

I want to tell you about the fun FB group I'm part of, together with many of your favourite authors.

Historical Harlots is a group where readers can win give-aways and many novel prizes!

Basically, it's a happy place offering readers lots of fun!

Check it out here!

LISTEN IN AUDIO - AT EBOOK PRICES!

Listen to the first of the series - **Rake's Honour** - in audio at e-book prices.

Also available are **Rogue's Kiss, The Honourable Fortune Hunter** and **The Wilful Widow**

Get them here!
www.beverleyoakley.com

ABOUT THE AUTHOR

Beverley was seventeen when she bundled up her first 500+ page romance and sent it to a publisher. Rejection followed swiftly. Drowning one's heroine on the last page, she was informed, was not in line with the expectations of romance readers.

So Beverley became a journalist.

After a whirlwind romance with a handsome Norwegian bush pilot she met in Botswana's beautiful Okavango Delta, Beverley discovered what real romance was all about, saved her heroine from a watery grave in her next manuscript and published her first romance in 2009.

Since then, she's written more than twenty-seven sweet to sizzling historical romances laced with mystery and intrigue under the name Beverley Oakley.

She also writes psychological historical mysteries, and Colonial-Africa-set romantic suspense, as Beverley Eikli.

With an inspiring view of a Gothic nineteenth-century insane asylum across the road, Beverley lives north of Melbourne with her gorgeous husband, two lovely daughters and a rambunctious Rhodesian Ridgeback called Mombo, named after the safari lodge where she and her husband met.

Visit Beverley's website - www.beverleyoakley.com - to sign up for her newsletter and receive a free book.
Join Beverley's reader group on Facebook

<u>Follow Beverley</u>
On Bookbub
On Goodreads
On Facebook

Please get in touch here:
www.beverley@eikli.com

And, if you enjoyed The Accidental Elopement, you can rate or review it here.